Sacrificed to Vanity

To my wonderful cousins,
Dwayne & Carol,
Love,
Karen

Karen Lucille Gross

WESTBOW
PRESS®
A DIVISION OF THOMAS NELSON
& ZONDERVAN

Scripture taken from the Holy Bible, NEW INTERNATIONAL VERSION®.
Copyright © 1973, 1978, 1984 by Biblica, Inc. All rights reserved worldwide.
Used by permission. NEW INTERNATIONAL VERSION® and NIV® are
registered trademarks of Biblica, Inc. Use of either trademark for the offering
of goods or services requires the prior written consent of Biblica US, Inc.

WestBow Press books may be ordered through booksellers or by contacting:

WestBow Press
A Division of Thomas Nelson & Zondervan
1663 Liberty Drive
Bloomington, IN 47403
www.westbowpress.com
1 (866) 928-1240

Because of the dynamic nature of the Internet, any web addresses or
links contained in this book may have changed since publication and may
no longer be valid. The views expressed in this work are solely those
of the author and do not necessarily reflect the views of the publisher,
and the publisher hereby disclaims any responsibility for them.

Any people depicted in stock imagery provided by Thinkstock are models,
and such images are being used for illustrative purposes only.
Certain stock imagery © Thinkstock.

ISBN: 978-1-5127-1295-7 (sc)
ISBN: 978-1-5127-1296-4 (e)

Library of Congress Control Number: 2015915155

Print information available on the last page.

WestBow Press rev. date: 9/29/2015

Chapter One

Seventeen-year-old Tracy Wilson gathered her books into her backpack as the long awaited last bell on Friday afternoon signaled freedom for the weekend. She exited the classroom and made her way through the crowded hallway to her locker, where her best friend Jordan Sanders was waiting.

"Finally!" Tracy sighed. "I thought this day would never . . ." but there her train of thought derailed. Jordan's quizzical expression was replaced by a nod of understanding as she followed Tracy's glance. Calista Dubois, the new girl at school, was working the crowded hallway as her personal red carpet. The jostling multitude of students parted like the Red Sea. Calista was followed by an entourage of girls all wearing identical expressions of practiced boredom.

Tracy couldn't imagine anyone with whom she had less in common. Calista was tall, slim, and styled just like the girls in the fashion magazine photos that covered the inside of her locker. Tracy would be thrilled to wear her flannel pj's and slippers to school, and the inside of her locker was covered with cute pictures of kittens and puppies.

The entourage came to a stop at Calista's locker, which just happened to be the one next to Tracy's. Jordan put her hand over her mouth and whispered, "Here we go again—and she has a bigger audience today."

"Caution, ladies—two Christians dead ahead," Calista addressed her flock like a tour guide. "Watch your language—they have virgin ears. Don't mention evolution—or we will be here for an hour debating creation and they still won't listen to reason. And whatever you do, don't tell them where tonight's party is happening! They might want to come, but I'm sure their mommies won't let them."

"Doesn't matter anyway. The bouncer would never let them in. Their fashion sense hasn't caught up with this millennium." This was from Joelle, a tall slender girl wearing skinny jeans.

Andrea, who grew up in the house across the street from Tracy and had known her and Jordan since preschool days taunted, "Even if they had clothes from this decade, they don't have the bods to wear them. Jordan has no waistline—she looks like a beach ball with arms and legs. And Tracy has obviously never been visited by the puberty fairy."

After the howls of laughter died down a bit, Andrea (who was also wearing skinny jeans), continued, "And even if they had decent party clothes and the bods to fill them out, their parents would never let them leave the house looking like that."

"Ooh, Calista, look!" Kristen, another tall slender girl wearing (you guessed it!) skinny jeans exclaimed. "The chubby one has red fingernail polish on!"

"Tsk, tsk, tsk!" Calista clicked her tongue as she walked around Tracy to examine Jordan's offensive fingernails. "Didn't your parents warn you that if God had meant for you to have red fingernails he would have made them that way?"

"God's gonna get you for that!" Andrea taunted.

"Her ears are pierced, too," Kristen said. "I'm pretty sure that's not allowed either. God didn't put no holes in Eve's ears."

"Not in Adam's ears, either—not even in one," Andrea added.

"Hey, Calista! Have you heard the one about why God created Adam before Eve?" This came from Monica, a slightly pudgy short girl who was also wearing skinny jeans, but should not have been. She was standing on tip toes at the periphery of the entourage, trying to make eye contact with Calista. Calista just rolled her eyes.

"I don't give a fig. Why don't you just leaf me alone!" Calista said, and a fresh wave of giggles filled the hallway.

"Actually," Monica continued, "That's close, but the answer is really . . ."

"Whatever!" Calista retorted, with a dismissive wave. "I thought you were religious too. Changing teams just to get close to me? I don't swing that way, sister!"

Tracy made brief eye contact with Monica, and tried unsuccessfully to smile. She and Monica had been good friends in the past. Monica's family used to attend the same church as Tracy and Jordan's families, so they had known each other pretty much since birth. Monica's parents divorced when she was seven, and they had stopped attending church before that, but the three girls remained friends until high school.

Lately Monica had changed. She ignored her old friends as she tried to gain acceptance by the popular students. She no longer professed any faith. She even joined in with Calista and the rest of the cool clique when they taunted Tracy and Jordan for being Christians.

The crowd around Calista's locker grew as students exiting the classrooms filled the hallway with laughter and noisy antics. Monica slunk her way through the crowded hallway and exited the building, humiliated by the raucous laughter that chased her out.

A tall, athletic-looking guy in a football jersey got Calista's attention and asked, "Are you coming to the party tonight? I could pick you up."

"No, let me pick you up!" A slightly shorter guy built like a linebacker literally scooped her up and started to carry her down the hall. "Girl, you've put on a couple of pounds since the last time I picked you up," he said as he set her down.

"Remind me to never hook up with you again!" Calista giggled. "By the way, what's your name?"

"Oh, that's cold, girl! How will you know what name to put on the birth certificate where it says 'Baby's Daddy'?"

"Calista would never have a baby with you, Danny Boy!" the first guy said. "I would personally escort her to the nearest abortion clinic if you knocked her up."

The two guys traded arm jabs and head slaps as the crowd jostled and elbowed their way to the exit doors. Suddenly Jordan and Tracy were alone in the silent hallway.

Jordan broke the silence. "O-o-kay then! I don't know how you can stand to have a locker next to hers!"

"I am trying to give her the benefit of the doubt. I'm sure that she must have been through some hard times in her life. So when she makes fun of me, I just keep reminding myself that deep down inside she is probably wounded and hurting. This queen bee persona is just an act that she puts on to make her feel better about herself."

"You know, you are really starting to talk like your mom." Jordan said.

"I will take that as a compliment, Jordie. My mom is my hero."

5

"I know what you mean, Tray. Your mom is my hero too. Do I really look like a beach ball with legs and arms?"

"Nah. You're just a bit slow in developing a waist. And what is it that your mom is always telling us?"

"You mean, 'A waist is a terrible thing to mind'?"

"That's the one, my dear. Now if you don't mind, I must go home to help my mom with the twins before she loses her mind."

Chapter Two

When Tracy got home from school, the house was quiet. She found her mother in the kitchen.

"Hi, Mom," she said, dropping her backpack on a chair. "The house is so quiet! Are both twins actually sleeping at the same time?"

Tracy's mom and dad—Kathryn and Alex Wilson—were foster parents, and they had recently taken in a set of nine month old twin boys with fetal alcohol syndrome. They also had a ten-year-old boy named Jeremy, whose drug-addicted mother was in rehab."

"Amazing isn't it?" Kathryn answered.

"Do all babies with FAS cry so much?"

"It is common. Thomas and Timothy's mother drank all throughout her pregnancy, so these little guys were born addicted and have had to go through withdrawal."

"Poor little guys! That's hard enough for grown-ups to deal with," Tracy said. "But I know that you were up most of the night with them, so why don't you go have a nap while I get supper going?"

"You are sounding so grown up yourself, my child. I will take you up on that offer. I sure could use a nap."

Kathryn turned and trudged toward her bedroom. Then she turned back towards the kitchen. "Oh, I almost forgot to tell you. We are getting a new fosterling today, a girl your age. Maybe you've met her at school: her name is Calista."

"No way, Mom!" Tracy exclaimed, "She's like this rich queen bee! She hates me! Isn't there anywhere else she could go?"

"No, there isn't. Plus she requested our home. This is her third pregnancy, and I counseled her at the center last year after her second abortion."

"Why can't she stay at the center?"

"We are full at the center. Plus she's only seventeen, so she qualifies for foster care."

"Maybe she just needs counseling. Why does she have to live here?"

"Tracy Marie Wilson! We don't pick and choose fosterlings! We are not picking out a puppy here. This is a girl who needs our help! Calista told the school nurse that her mother threatened to kick her out of the house if she won't abort. Now, somebody generously offered to start supper so that I could have a nap."

"Okay, Mom. You're right, I did offer."

"And right after supper you need to clean your room. Calista will be bunking with you."

"Share my *room* with Calista? Seriously, Mom?"

"Yes, *seriously*, Tracy. Just think of this as an opportunity to practice grace and hospitality."

As her mother went for a nap, Tracy went to the kitchen to peel potatoes. "I wish we were picking out a puppy," she said to no one. "Or a kitten. Yes, I think I would much rather be sharing my bedroom with a kitten."

Chapter Three

-Twelve Weeks Pregnant

Calista arrived late that evening, with three large suitcases and a sour expression on her face. She settled onto the extra bed in Tracy's room and turned to face the wall. Tracy was at a loss for words. What do you say to someone who hates you and will be sharing your bedroom for an indeterminate amount of time?

"Don't those babies ever stop crying?" Calista mumbled.

"Not for long," Tracy answered.

"Is there something wrong with them?"

"Yes," Tracy said. "They have fetal alcohol syndrome. Their mother drank while she was pregnant."

"And that's why they cry like that?" Calista sat up in bed, but continued staring at the wall. "I guess your parents told you that I'm pregnant."

"Yeah, they did."

"I want to keep this baby." Calista continued. "I suppose they also told you that I've had two abortions, and my mom wants me to abort this one too?"

"Yeah, they told me that too. My mom works with the League for Life."

"That's why they brought me here. I want to keep this baby. But you had better keep your mouth shut at school. Everybody here will know about me soon enough, if I don't abort this time. I want to enjoy at least a couple of months before everyone in this front-porch-swinging, busy-body town starts wagging their tongues about me."

"I won't say anything at school," Tracy promised. "We have a Wilson family adage that we don't gossip about our fosterlings."

"What's an adage?"

"It's like a cross between a rule and a vow. My mother is very poetic."

"Whatever. Just make sure that no one finds out I am staying here. I would never hear the end of it." Calista lay back on the bed and drew the covers up over her head. Feeling somewhat dismissed, Tracy left the room.

Upstairs, both twins were still crying, so Tracy figured her parents could use some help in the nursery. Maybe they would let her move a cot in so she could bunk with the babies while Calista was here.

11

Chapter Four

Tracy woke up with a stiff neck from falling asleep in the rocking chair. Little Thomas was snuggled up against her shoulder, finally sleeping like a baby. *Sleeping like a baby* - ha! Whoever came up with that expression had obviously never lived in a house with a baby.

She got up carefully without waking Thomas and successfully transferred the sleeping baby to his crib. Timothy was asleep too. Yeah! She briefly entertained the idea of grabbing a blanket and pillow and sleeping on the floor, but she already felt stiff and wanted her bed.

The house was quiet. Tracy couldn't remember a time when everyone was asleep at the same time. She glanced at the kitchen clock. It was only 1:30. Surely Calista would still be awake. She couldn't imagine a teenager sleeping by 1:30 on a Friday night. The Wilsons weren't very strict about bedtimes or curfews. They so often had babies in the house that woke up several times during the night, plus her mom dabbled in writing, and rarely found time during the day.

Tracy went downstairs where there was a game room, a TV corner, a library nook, a bathroom, a little kitchenette, and two large bedrooms. All of the lights were on, but it was quiet. She checked Jeremy's room, and saw that the ten-year-old was asleep with a Godzilla toy in one hand and a T-Rex in the other. She smiled as she pulled the covers over his little body and kissed his forehead. He was such a little cutie. He had gained a couple of pounds since he came, but he was still small for his age.

Jeremy's mom was a single parent, and a drug addict. The poor little guy had already been in four foster homes. Every time his mom went through rehab and got her life back together, she would convince the social workers that she was fit to be a parent again, and Jeremy would be returned 'home'. The longest of his mom's clean stints lasted less than a year. She would invariably find a new boyfriend who would suck her back into the chaotic world that accompanied drug use.

Tracy turned off the light in Jeremy's room and prayed a quick prayer for the courage to face her new roommate.

What Tracy found when she opened her bedroom door was a chaotic mess, but no Calista. It looked like the three huge suitcases had projectile vomited their contents all over the room.

Tracy thought for a moment that Calista could be hiding underneath one of the piles of clothes on the floor, but she quickly remembered that she was not looking for a child, but a seventeen-year-old pregnant fashionista with perfect hair and make-up. But if this was how Calista lived, Tracy wondered how she could look so put-together every day.

Once Tracy was able to look away from the piles of stuff on the floor, she noticed the open window and the chair in front of the window. Then she remembered that the kids at school had been talking about picking up Calista for a party. Just when her parents were finally getting some much needed sleep, Tracy was going to have to wake them.

Chapter Five

As it turned out, Tracy didn't need to wake her parents. The doorbell rang and woke everyone in the house. Both babies started screaming, and Jeremy ran to Tracy's room, crying and shaking. She scooped up the little boy, who still grasped Godzilla and the T-Rex, and carried him upstairs to see what was going on.

Kathryn was holding Thomas and Timothy, and Tracy's dad Alex was talking to two uniformed police officers at the front door. They were saying something about a party and underage drinking, and they wanted to know if Calista Dubois was supposed to be in the care of the Wilsons. The social worker who had brought Calista to their home just a few hours ago was back.

And so was Calista. Her hair and make-up were no longer looking so perfect. Her dress was torn, and she was missing the heel of one shoe. She was three sheets to the wind, drunk as a sailor, and swearing like one too. She could barely stand up, so the social worker took her by the arm and led her to a couch to sit down. Alex went outside to talk with the officers. Kathryn went to the nursery to put the twins back in their cribs. Jeremy went back to bed.

Tracy wasn't sure what to do. The social worker, Sadie Nelson, beckoned for her to sit down beside her. Awkward.

After an uncomfortable ten minutes of listening to Calista's incoherent mumblings, Kathryn came back with a tea tray. Tracy wondered how her mother could be so cheerful and congenial at two in the morning.

"Oh, thank you, Kathryn," Sadie said as she poured herself a cup of tea. "I don't know how you do it—but I am sure glad you do. You had better have a cup too, Calista. You have a lot of explaining to do. What were you thinking, going off to a party and drinking in your condition?"

Calista responded to the social worker's reprimand with a sudden spewage of vomit. Kathryn was ready for that response. She quickly picked up the bowl that the Wilson family referred to as the 'barf bucket' and had it expertly positioned just in time. With her free hand, she held back Calista's hair.

Just then Alex came back inside. "They've released Calista into our custody, at least for tonight so she can sleep this off." he announced. "Those two officers said they probably won't be charging her with anything, but I might have to take Calista to the police department tomorrow morning to give a statement. There may be an investigation to find out who sold or gave alcohol to six underage girls, and served them enough to get them all extremely intoxicated."

"Well she is certainly in no condition to answer any questions tonight," Kathryn said. "I'll take her to the bathroom and help her get cleaned up. Alex, could you set up a cot in my office? I would like to keep an eye on Calista tonight. Hopefully she'll throw up enough that her baby won't be harmed by the alcohol. Tracy, go get some sleep. I am going to need your help in the morning."

Tracy was exhausted. She gave her mom a quick hug and said good night to her dad and to Sadie. It had been a long day.

Chapter Six

Kathryn sat at the large antique scroll top desk that dominated her office space. Her new lap top seemed so small on the huge desk surface compared to her old computer with the separate monitor, keyboard, and hard drive that used to sit here along with all of the disks and manuals. She marveled at how fast technology was changing—and then she felt old for thinking that way. At least now there was more space on, in, and under this beautiful desk she inherited from her grandfather. For the first time in years, she could scroll the top of the desk down—to hide the mess and keep her confidential paper work out of sight.

As quietly as she could, Kathryn finished typing up her anecdotal report of Calista's first day in her care. Not a great start. This girl was going to be a challenge. "*Am I strong enough for this challenge, Lord?*" The still small voice that she was finally starting to recognize as God reminded her that He was the one who brought this lost lamb into her home, and He would provide the strength and wisdom that she would need each day.

Calista stirred on the cot in the dimly lit room and Kathryn studied the girl's face. Without the make-up and the attitude, she looked so sweet. Teenagers were a little like babies that way: a lot cuter when they were asleep.

Kathryn offered a silent prayer of thanks for Tracy, her only biological child, who would be turning eighteen this summer. She thanked God for his indescribable mercy in allowing her to give life and be a mother to this special child. The years were going by so fast! Her little girl was becoming a beautiful young woman. Tracy was such a blessing: she worked hard and got good grades at school; she had a soft heart and a gentle spirit; and was always ready to help others. She was full of self confidence without being full of herself. More than all of that, she loved God and had a bold, personal faith.

Kathryn's prayers moved on to intercession for the fosterlings under her care. She prayed for Timothy and Thomas, who had been in the Wilson home since they were two months old. The twin boys had been abandoned by their alcoholic mother in a public restroom at the hospital. A nurse working the night shift discovered the two babies in a pool of blood on the floor, and rushed them up to the NICU unit. She alerted hospital security to look for the mother. They followed the trail of blood from the restroom, down the hallway, and then out through the front exit. Unfortunately, at the end of the trail, the security guards discovered the mother's body behind a dumpster. It was determined that she had died of alcohol poisoning.

Kathryn prayed that the police would soon identify the mother so that they could look for the next of kin. Much as she loved the little guys, she did not want for them to have to grow up in foster care. The sooner a permanent placement could be made, the better.

Then there was Jeremy. His drug addicted mother loved him dearly, and wanted to have him back. He had been with the Wilsons for about six months now, and according to Sadie, the mother had almost completed another court ordered rehab. Kathryn prayed that Jeremy and his mother could be a family again. After all the boy had been through in his ten years, his was a fragile soul. Every night he prayed that his mother could have the courage to give up her drugs and her abusive boyfriends so he could go home.

Kathryn's prayers for her fosterlings always moved her to tears. She didn't want to disturb Calista now that she was finally sleeping. The teen had been vomiting profusely until four in the morning, and Kathryn had been by her side: holding her hair back, getting her to take sips of ginger ale, sponging the sweat off her face, and shushing her so the twins in the nursery on the other side of the wall would not wake up again. She wondered how much alcohol the girl must have consumed to be this sick. Most likely, there had been drugs at the party as well.

Exhausted and spent, Kathryn finally turned off the dim office lamp, and went to bed. She sent up a quick prayer for a few hours of sleep before it would be time to get up and do it all again.

Chapter Seven

Tracy knew it had to happen eventually. Calista couldn't sleep forever. Tracy was pretty sure she would not have to face her new roomie before noon. But it was at least four o'clock in the afternoon before an unkempt version of Calista Dubois made a tentative appearance in the kitchen.

"Where's your mom?" she mumbled in a gravelly voice as she stumbled to a chair.

"She went to the grocery store," Tracy said. She was holding Timothy and doing a bouncy dance around the kitchen, to try to soothe the colicky nine month-old. Thomas was doing a bouncy dance of his own, content for the moment to sit in a baby bouncer chair on the toy strewn kitchen floor. Jeremy was sitting on the floor, playing with toy cars.

"What kind of place is this anyway? How many babies are there? Is this some kind of black market baby selling mill or something? And don't those babies ever shut up?" After her rapid fire questions, Calista folded her arms on the table and rested her head.

Tracy couldn't help but laugh, but she quickly stifled the impulse. Calista must have a ginormous headache, and the twins had been especially cranky all day. "Okay. This is a foster home. We have two babies right now, and Jeremy who is ten. No we don't sell babies, and no, the twins are rarely both quiet at the same time. Anything else?"

"Yeah, where are your cats?"

"Our cats?"

"Yeah, your school locker is plastered with pictures of cats. I've always figured that your house would be full of cats."

"I am not allowed to have a cat. One of the fosterlings might be allergic."

"Fosterlings?"

"That's what my mom calls the foster children who live here. Speaking of my mom, she just pulled in." Tracy breathed a silent *Thank You* prayer that this awkward conversation was over.

Chapter Eight

"Hi kids, I'm back," Kathryn breezed in, carrying at least four very full reusable cloth grocery bags. "There are more bags in the back of the van. Tracy, where's your father? Calista—you're up. Good. How are you feeling? Here, Tracy—trade." Kathryn set the grocery bags on the counter and reached her arms to take Timothy, who immediately stopped fussing.

"How do you do that, Mom?" Tracy asked. "I think Dad's in his office—or maybe not..."

Tracy's father Alex (who worked from home as a legal consultant), was sneaking up behind Kathryn, shushing Timothy, who was now giggling. "Honey, could you go get the rest of the groceries? I need to get these things put away and then get started on dinner," Kathryn said without looking back, as she handed the baby back to Tracy. Timothy promptly resumed crying. Thomas, who had been playing happily, now joined his twin brother in a wailing rhapsody. Kathryn scooped up Thomas, sniffed his bottom end, and handed the smelly baby to Alex.

"Change of plans. I will get the rest of the groceries. Alex, Tracy, take the twins to the nursery and get them cleaned up; Jeremy, Sweetie Pie— could you go help them, please? Calista—you can help me get the groceries."

Kathryn started a silent prayer for wisdom. "*God, you love this lost lamb. You also love the new little one you are knitting inside her. Please give me wisdom and strength.*"

Maybe she was getting too old for this. She couldn't remember the last time she had slept more than four or five hours at a time. Between babies waking up at night, toddlers waking up at the crack of dawn, and teens staying out until the wee hours; sleep was a precious commodity at the Wilson home.

Besides parenting fosterlings, Kathryn worked as a counselor at a crisis pregnancy center called House of Grace. Alex often said Kathryn loved her work so much she had to take it home with her. It was true. Kathryn's heart broke whenever she had to turn anyone away, but the residential center only had room for six women at a time. She helped as many women as she could with the limited resources of the center, but she knew that some of the women she counseled would make the choice to visit the abortion clinic on the corner—a choice she sadly conceded was legally theirs to make.

So Kathryn and Alex made the decision to become foster parents. They took in children of all ages, but Kathryn had a soft spot in her heart for pregnant teens. Calista was the fourth to live with them. Of the first three, two had given their babies up for adoption and one chose to keep her baby.

Calista broke the silence of Kathryn's reverie. "What am I supposed to call you?" she asked. Kathryn realized that she had been lost in thought. "Sorry, what did you say?" Calista repeated the question.

"You can call me Mama Kate," Kathryn answered.

"Well Mama Kate, when are you going to give me what's coming for last night?"

"What are you expecting to come?"

"A punishment of some sort, I guess. I don't know. Are you going to ground me, or kick me out?"

"What would we accomplish by grounding you or kicking you out?"

Calista looked around, confused. "I guess it would teach me not to sneak out and drink while I am pregnant, or something."

"Don't you know why you should not go out and drink while you are pregnant?"

Now Calista was really confused. "I don't know . . . I guess . . . it would be bad for the baby?"

"It sounds to me like you already know that."

"Then why did you let me do it?"

Kathryn stifled a smile. "I don't recall giving you permission. In fact, I don't think you even asked."

"You would have said no."

"So, then you thought it would be better to just go ahead and do it, and ask for forgiveness later?

"Yes . . . but . . . no . . ." Calista sputtered. "You wouldn't have given me permission . . ."

Kathryn was praying hard. She knew from a whole lot of experience that if you want a teen to act like an adult you had to treat them as adults even when they were acting like children. "So how would my punishing you help you to learn a lesson that you already know?"

Calista wasn't used to adults who treated her this way. "Because . . . you're like . . . a mom . . . but you're not acting like a mom. A mom wouldn't let me get away with stuff like that."

Kathryn's heart was pounding, but she knew that this was a critical moment. She lowered her voice a little. "Calista, you are not a child anymore, so I am not going to treat you like a child. Adults get to make their own decisions, but then they have to live with the consequences of their choices. Tell me honestly: which would make you stop sneaking off to go drinking – getting grounded for the next six months, or living the rest of your life knowing that your child has brain damage because you got away with drinking while you were pregnant?"

Calista was speechless. Just at that moment Alex and Tracy came back to the kitchen with the twins and Jeremy. The lesson was over, for now.

Chapter Nine

Tracy felt like a lifetime had happened since she got home from school on Friday. Was it really only a day and a half ago that Calista was just a popular girl at school who picked on her at the lockers? Now she was sharing a bedroom with the Queen Bee, who was pregnant, who snuck out the window to go to a party, got totally blotto, and was brought home by the police at two in the morning. Had all of that happened in the last thirty-six hours?

Calista had been sent down to clean up Tracy's bedroom and she had actually done a pretty good job of it—despite objections that she couldn't possibly be expected to do chores in her condition and that there wasn't enough space in the closet and the room was too small and too full of Tracy's stuff and why did the Wilsons take her in if they didn't have room for her?

In response to Calista's complaints, Alex put up a temporary wall dividing Tracy's bedroom, with a closet rod on Calista's side. He put up a door that locked on Calista's side, so she could have some privacy, although she would have to go through Tracy's side of the room to get to the hallway. Each room had a window large enough to get out in case of fire, Alex told the girls, but he didn't recommend that either of them should get in the habit of using the window as a door.

"Your dad is a bit dorky," Calista remarked from her side of the room when the girls were getting ready for bed.

"That he is." Tracy agreed.

"But he is pretty handy. I doubt that any of my stepdads could have built a wall in a couple of hours."

"How many stepdads have you had?"

"Three if you're just counting the ones my mom was married to. There have been quite a few that she just lived with."

"How about your biological father, if you don't mind my asking?"

"I've never met him. According to my mom: she met and married my dad while she was working in Paris as a nanny. She was fifteen and he was eighteen. His parents were insanely wealthy, he was their only child, and they threatened to disinherit him unless he had the marriage to the American girl annulled. He was so distraught that he jumped off a bridge into the River Thames and drowned."

"No way! That is an incredible story!"

"Yeah. But that's all it is: just a story. My mom lies about everything. She lives in a fantasy world. I'll bet I was conceived under the bleachers in some high school gym, and Mom just made up the Paris thing so that my grandparents wouldn't have a cow when she came home pregnant. One flaw in her story was that she always said it was the River Thames where he drowned, but even I know that the Thames runs through London, not Paris. Her parents were religious, and would have disowned her, so she made up that story and even changed her name. She used to be Cheryl Brown. Now she is Marcelle Dubois."

"Wow," Tracy said. "I had no idea. You have had quite the life."

"Your life is way weirder. I don't know of anyone my age that still lives with both bio-parents. And all those babies? Do you get a lot of money for taking them in?"

Tracy laughed. "No, not much! My parents just do it . . . actually I'm not sure why. But they have been foster parents for a long time. I can't remember not having fosterlings in the house. Now go to sleep. We have to get up for church tomorrow."

"Church?" Calista choked out. "They won't make me go, will they?"

"Not if you don't want to. But it's not that bad. I have a lot of friends there, like Jordan. You've met her. Your friend described her as a beach ball with arms and legs."

Calista chortled. "That was funny. It's a good description of her."

"And I have apparently not had a visit by the puberty fairy godmother yet . . ."

Calista snorted. "That's hilarious! You are really weird!"

"Good night, Calista."

"Good night, you little weirdo!"

As Tracy turned out the light, she prayed a silent prayer: "*Lord, please help me get through these next six months without killing her.*"

Chapter Ten

Calista did not attend church with the Wilson family the next morning. She was still sleeping when they got home after church. Tracy asked if she could go to Jordan's place for a sleep over, "to give Calista a little space." Kathryn told her to go ahead, but remember the Wilson Family Adage # 2: *No gossiping about the fosterlings.*

That one would be a challenge with this particular fosterling, Tracy knew, especially with Jordan. Tracy wasn't even supposed to tell anyone who was staying in her home. That would be tough—especially since Tracy and Jordan usually walked to school together. She couldn't quite imagine Calista wanting to walk with them. Did Calista have a car? The high school was only a ten minute walk from the Wilson home; Tracy couldn't imagine her parents driving her to school every day.

Jordan knew Tracy too well, though. She had barely stepped inside when Jordan grabbed her arm and dragged her into her bedroom and closed the door. "Okay, spill, Tray!"

"Whatever are you talking about, Jordie?"

"You think I can't tell when you are keeping something from me? You could hardly make eye contact with me all morning at church. Out with it!"

"You know I can't tell you. Fosterling confidentiality. Wilson Family Adage #2.

"So, it's about someone staying at your house. I thought you guys were full already."

"Well legally, we can have up to six kids, including me. We just don't have that many bedrooms. So I have to share my room with her."

"That rules out a hot guy. I know your parents wouldn't let you share your room with a hot guy."

"Or a cold guy, either . . . or whatever the opposite of 'hot' is, when you're using 'hot' as an adjective to modify a guy. That reminds me, have you studied for the English test tomorrow? I brought my books along so I could study today."

"Way to change the subject, Tray! And why would you have to study for an English test? You know you always ace them."

"That's because I study."

"You are really not going to tell me, are you? Some best friend you are."

"Sorry. But you know that a Wilson Family Adage trumps best friend."

Chapter Eleven

Monday morning was bound to come, sooner or later. Tracy didn't have to wait long to find out how bad this situation was going to get. She was getting ready for first period when Calista showed up without her obsequious entourage. She came up behind Tracy, spun her around, and slammed her up against the lockers.

"You little snitch!" Calista screamed. "What happened to your Wilson Family Creed or whatever you call it?"

"I have no idea what you are talking about, honest!"

"Your holier-than-thou no gossip rule!" Calista poked a finger into Tracy's chest. "Everyone in the school knows about me being pregnant and staying in your foster house!"

By this time, Calista's tirade had drawn a crowd. Tracy was just sputtering a protest when the bell for first period chimed. The crowd thinned as a few students went to class, but most stayed in the hallway to see what was going on.

The next thing Tracy knew, the vice principal, Mr. Keller, was ushering her and Calista into his office. "Okay girls, what's going on here?"

"She promised me she wouldn't tell! Her family even has this religious commandment thing because, oh, they are such good church people! They will take you in, and they love babies so much, they will protect you from your mother who wants you to have an abortion and your secrets are safe with them. But then you go there, and the next thing you know—the whole school knows everything!"

"I didn't understand any of that, Calista," the vice principal said. "Tracy, can you explain what she is talking about?"

"I don't think so, sir. But you know, my family is a foster family," Tracy said. "Calista is living with us. But I don't know what she is talking about. I didn't tell anyone anything! Honest. My mother would kill me for gossiping about a fosterling!"

Just then the school secretary buzzed. Mr. Keller picked up the phone, listened for a moment, and then said, "Send them in please." He opened the door and ushered in Kathryn Wilson and Sadie Nelson, the social worker.

"Mom, how did you get here so fast?" Tracy asked.

A few seconds passed as everyone looked confused. Kathryn broke the silence. "I didn't know you were going to call the girls in for this meeting."

Now even Mr. Keller looked a bit confused. The school secretary, who had been standing behind Kathryn cleared her throat, and then chimed in, "Miss Nelson called just after 8:00 this morning to request a meeting with you, regarding Calista's situation. I took the liberty of adding it to your schedule, and I was going to let you know when you got in, but when I saw that Tracy and Calista were with you, I assumed that you knew Mrs. Wilson and Miss Nelson were coming in."

"No," Mr. Keller said. "I was a bit late this morning, and there was a kerfuffle in the hallway by the lockers. Miss Dubois and Miss Wilson were involved in an altercation, so I escorted them here to see what was going on. Why don't we all have a seat and see if we can get this sorted out. Miss Nelson, you called for a meeting?"

"Yes sir," Sadie began. "My office received a call on Friday afternoon from your school nurse. Calista had confided to her that she was pregnant, and that her mother was threatening to kick her out of the home unless she had an abortion. So I placed her with the Wilsons, since Kathryn is active with the pro life group. I requested an appointment with you this morning so that you would be apprised of the situation."

"You said something about an altercation?" Kathryn asked. "What was going on?"

Calista had been on the edge of her seat, waiting to jump into the conversation. "Everybody knows I am pregnant and that I am staying with you! She told everyone!" In her fury, Calista got up and pointed at Tracy. "I thought you had some kind of family code that you don't gossip about people!"

"Tracy, did you tell someone that Calista was staying with us?" Kathryn asked.

"No, Mom! Honest, I didn't say anything!" Tracy protested.

"Then how did everyone know?" Calista accused.

"Are you sure you didn't tell Jordan anything?" Kathryn asked.

"No, Mom! I didn't tell Jordan anything!"

Mr. Keller broke in, "So what exactly happened this morning?"

"Somebody put a coat hanger in my locker!"

Mr. Keller looked confused again. "That's a little odd, and it is disconcerting that someone broke into your locker, but why would a coat hanger bother you?"

"It came with a note that said, 'Here, you might need this. Those Wilson Neanderthals won't give you a choice.' Somebody opened my locker and put that in."

Mr. Keller didn't look any less confused. "That is very unfortunate, and we will do everything we can to find out who did that. But how does this lead to everyone knowing your situation?"

"Well, duh! Everybody follows me around all day. When I opened my locker, they all saw the coat hanger and the note."

Kathryn gave voice to the obvious. "What makes you think Tracy had anything to do with this?"

"She's the only one who knew where I was staying."

"What about whoever took you to that party on Friday?" Sadie asked.

"I'm not that stupid, Miss Nelson," Calista snapped. "I met them at a coffee shop. Wait a minute though—how did I get back to your house after the party?"

"You mean to say you don't remember the police taking you home?" Sadie asked. "Didn't you talk to Mr. and Mrs. Wilson about the party?"

"Mama Kate, I mean, Mrs. Wilson, talked to me about it the next day. But she didn't punish me."

Sadie looked over at Kathryn. "Do you mean to say that there were no consequences for sneaking out to go to a party and getting drunk?"

Mr. Keller cleared his throat. "Ahem. I think these girls should be getting back to their classes."

Chapter Twelve

As Kathryn and Sadie were leaving Mr. Keller's office, Sara Belanger, the school nurse, stopped them. "Do the two of you have a moment?"

"Sure," Kathryn said. Sadie nodded. Sara asked them to step into her office.

"What's up?" Sadie asked as she took a seat in the nurse's office.

"I understand Calista was escorted home by the police late Friday night."

"More like early Saturday morning, but yes," Sadie answered.

"Was she very ill when she got home, for about twenty-four hours?" the nurse inquired.

"Yes, she was," Kathryn replied. "She was vomiting profusely, for most of that night."

"She was very drunk," Sadie interjected.

"The thing is," Sara continued, "All of the girls from our school who were at that party were very sick when they got home, except for one. Most of the parents assumed they were drunk. But one of the girls came to see me this morning. She said

39

they each had only one beer at the party, except for Monica, who had at least three."

"I think that Calista had more than one beer that night. She was hardly able to stand up," Kathryn said. "And she said this morning that she didn't even remember being brought home by the police."

"Andrea, the girl who came to see me this morning, said she has often had way more to drink, and has never been this sick from beer. She was curious about why Monica was the only one of their group who didn't get sick at the party."

"So maybe the girls who got sick were doing more than drinking beer," Sadie suggested.

"I thought of that too," Sara said. "But Andrea said she and the other girls were not taking any drugs. She said they weren't even smoking pot. She came to see me to ask if I thought it was possible that someone slipped something into their drinks. She was suspicious of Monica, especially since she was pretty sure it was Monica who called the police that night."

Kathryn spoke up. "Now that you mentioned police, I just remembered that Alex mentioned something about one of the officers telling him they were releasing Calista into our care to sleep off the intoxication, but one of us would need to bring her in the next morning to give a statement. But then in the morning, the other officer called and told Alex they were not investigating after all, and they didn't need Calista to come. It all seemed a bit wonky."

"Well, you saved me a phone call by coming in this morning. I was especially concerned for Calista, being pregnant."

"Do you think the girls may have been given a date rape drug?" Kathryn furrowed her brow.

"That's the theory Andrea had. She also said she doesn't remember how she got home. I examined her, and didn't find any bruising to indicate rape. And unfortunately, most of the drugs that are considered to be 'rape drugs' don't stay in the bloodstream long enough to be detected."

"What do you know about Monica?" Kathryn asked.

"Not much. Andrea told me she is unpopular, and she follows Calista around like a puppy even when Calista tells her to get lost."

"So the million dollar question then is why Monica went to that party," Kathryn surmised. "Do you know anything about her parents?"

"Just what is on file at the office," Sara said while getting her computer going. "Parents have to fill out paperwork every year to let the school know essential information like which parents have restraining orders, what custody arrangements families have, the surnames of siblings or step siblings who also attend this school, which students have life threatening allergies and carry epi pens, which students are pregnant, or already have children, and then we need signed parental permission forms to dispense ibuprofen or acetaminophen. . ." the nurse paused for a breath, consulted her computer and continued, "Okay, then. Monica Lutz . . . parents divorced . . . that's not unusual. Amicable joint custody . . . oh, this is unusual. It says here that Monica was legally adopted by her mother's new husband a few months ago. You don't often see kids taking on a stepfather's last name at this age. Her surname is now Johnson. Her new father is Charlie Johnson, occupation: police officer. Does that help at all?"

Sadie said, "Charlie Johnson—that name sounds familiar. I should know who that is, but I can't remember. Hm. Kathryn, does that name ring any bells for you?"

"I don't think so," Kathryn answered. "The name Monica Lutz does, though. If I am thinking of the same person, she was in Tracy's Sunday School class way back when. I don't think the family came to church very often. As I recall, they stopped coming altogether when the parents split up and the mother remarried. So it is probably not the same family. I can't remember the last name of the mother's new husband, but I'm pretty sure it wasn't Johnson."

Chapter Thirteen

Leaving the office together was awkward. Tracy wanted to say something, but she didn't know what. Fortunately, their respective classes were in opposite directions. Calista stomped off, leaving Tracy without the opportunity.

First period was almost over by the time Tracy got there. She had totally forgotten about the English test. She had to write the test over lunch, so she didn't get a chance to see Jordan until the end of the school day. They met up at Jordan's locker instead of Tracy's.

"So, Wilson Family Adage #2 doesn't apply anymore after the cat's out of the bag, right?" Jordan asked.

"Does everyone know?"

"It's a small town, Tray, and no one else has family adages."

"Not that you know of."

"Nah—pretty sure your family is the only one."

"You could be right on that one, Jordie."

"So this was what you couldn't tell me on Sunday? That Calista Dubois, the most popular girl at school, is pregnant and staying at your house?"

"She is also sharing my room."

"Wow! That is so epic!"

"Epic it is."

"So the two of you are besties now, and pretty soon you'll be doing each other's hair and borrowing clothes?"

"Not a chance! She's like, five foot ten, and about a size 4; and I am not. I rather doubt that any of her clothes would fit me even if she would let me borrow them. My dad had to build a wall to divide my room, so that he could build a huge closet on her side of the wall."

"Wonder what she will do with all of those clothes once she gets a baby bump? Your dad will have to build an extension to her closet for maternity clothes soon."

"She will probably be one of those girls who just looks as if she swallowed a beach ball, and when her baby is born she will be able to wear her jeans home from the hospital."

"Do you mean her skinny jeans?"

"I don't think she has any other style."

Chapter Fourteen

The next day at lunchtime, Tracy and Jordan sat at their usual corner table. Calista and her skinny jean clad gang were a little quieter than usual. A hush fell over the cafeteria when they walked in. That was followed by whispered conversations and snickering from almost every table. As Calista walked to her usual table, the whispers and giggles got louder, and almost every eye in the room was following her.

Tracy knew there was something up. A loud gasp from Calista confirmed her suspicions. Students all over the room were looking at smart phones, tablets, laptops and other electronic gizmos. Calista threw her lunch tray down, and marched over to Tracy's table. She threw her phone at Tracy and shouted, "Look at what you started!" and to the room in general, she added, "I hate you all! Just leave me alone!"

As Calista began to storm out of the cafeteria, several of her flock got up to go with her. Turning to face them, she screamed, "Just leave me alone!

Stop following me!" Then with a dramatic pirouette, she whirled around and with head held high, she left the room. An awkward lull took over the room briefly before normal lunchroom chatter resumed as if nothing out of the ordinary happened.

Jordan and Tracy shared a moment of stunned silence before they noticed Calista's smart phone on the table in front of them. It was opened to a Facebook page dedicated to *Calista's Choices*. It featured an opinion poll for the question "Should Calista Abort?" There was a wager on how many months Calista would go this time before heading back to the abortion clinic and speculation on the identity of the baby daddy. Whoever started all of this knew details about Calista's past that Tracy hadn't known.

"I guess it is safe to assume that anyone who didn't know about Calista yesterday definitely knows now," Jordan remarked.

"That would be a safe assumption."

"Epic!"

"Epic it is," Tracy said. "I think we need to go and find her before she does something crazy."

"What, like run off to get drunk or high or something?" Jordan asked.

"Or worse, she could try to hurt herself and/or the baby."

"Do you think she is suicidal?"

"I don't know. We really don't know her all that well."

"Do you think she might go and get an abortion?"

"I have no idea. Don't they cost a lot of money?"

"I thought you said her family was rich."

"I said I thought her family must be rich. She has a lot of nice clothes and expensive shoes. You should have seen the floor of my room when she dumped out three huge suitcases full of clothes. Actually—you couldn't see the floor of my room. But that doesn't necessarily mean that her family is rich. I shouldn't have said that. I think I have been in violation of Wilson Family Adage #2 again."

"One of these days you should tell me what all of those adages are. How many are there anyway?"

"Five. Remind me one of these days to email you a copy. I think I should go to the office to call home and tell Mom and/or Dad that Calista might have run off again."

"Calista's phone is right here."

"I don't think I should use it without asking."

"How are you going to ask? She doesn't have her phone with her."

"Good point. Do you have your phone on you?"

"My brother has it today. We have to share. Seriously, we are like the only kids in this school who don't have our own phones. Look around, everybody else in this room is talking on a phone!"

"I guess I could use Calista's phone. After all, she did throw it at us. How do you turn it on?"

"I think it is on. Try pressing that green icon."

"Ok. Oops! I opened her contact list. Now she will really be ticked! Well—the first contact is 'Mom'. How do I get back to the main menu?"

"You are talking to the only other person in this room who doesn't know! Try pressing the green button again."

Tracy pressed the green icon again, and a woman's voice said, "Calista?" Tracy almost jumped out of her skin! She looked over at Jordan for help, but Jordan just shrugged her shoulders. So she said a tentative, "Hello?" into the phone.

"Did you get it done?" asked the woman on the phone. "Calista, are you there? Are you high? You sound high. I told you not to call me when you're high."

"Um, this isn't Calista . . ."

"Then who is this?"

"Um, this is, uh, Tracy Wilson. Calista is staying with us. Um, my family is the foster family that took her in . . .

"Why do you have Calista's phone? Where is she?"

"Calista threw her phone at me because of a Facebook page that someone made about her, um, her being pregnant and stuff. She was, um, upset and she ran off."

"Well, I hope she's gone to get rid of that kid. It'll just mess up her life if she tries to keep it. I should know. I was only fifteen when I had her, it ruined my figure, and I had a kid to take care of for the next eighteen years. So I've paid for Calista's abortions—and I gave her money for this one too. She should be grateful—no one gave me money to have an abortion. My mother was one of those pro-lifers that think we should all just have our babies and give up our lives. Is Calista still determined to keep that baby? Well, she can't say I didn't warn her. I will not give up my life to raise another kid, so if she has it, she's on her own. You tell her that I warned her! Now, why are you calling me?"

"Um, I called you by mistake. I'm really sorry, but I was trying to use Calista's phone, and I accidently called you. Sorry ..." and then the call ended. Tracy put down the phone like it was hot. She looked over at Jordan. "That didn't go particularly well," she said.

"Not particularly, no," Jordan agreed.

Chapter Fifteen

Tracy went to the office to use the pay phone to call home. Alex answered with his cheery, "Wilson residence!" Tracy's dad was a legal assistant and worked mostly from home so that Kathryn could work part time as a counselor at a crisis pregnancy center.

"Hi Dad! Is Calista there?" Tracy asked.

"No, she isn't. Is she supposed to be here?"

"Yes . . . I mean, no—she is not supposed to be there. I was just hoping she was."

"You've lost me there, Pumpkin."

"Is Mom home?"

"No, she is meeting with Sadie about Jeremy. Apparently his mom is out of rehab and wants to take him home. What's the problem with Calista?"

"I think she has run off somewhere. I'll come home right away and explain in person. Could you phone Sadie and let her know that Calista might be missing?"

"Sure thing."

"And Dad?"

"Yes, Pumpkin?"

"Pray!"

"Without ceasing, Pumpkin. Always pray without ceasing."

Chapter Sixteen

It took Tracy eight minutes to run home. By that time, Alex had called Sadie's office to tell them that Calista was missing; and Sadie and Kathryn were on their way home.

When they all met up at the Wilson home, Alex asked Tracy to explain what was going on. She showed them the Facebook page that someone set up to expose Calista.

"Why would someone do this?" Tracy asked. "What motivation would they have to trash Calista's reputation?"

"It could be someone who is jealous of her popularity. The anonymity of the internet makes people say things they would never say in person." Kathryn said.

"It looks like someone who knows a lot about her," Sadie said. "I will have to look through her file and see if there is anyone from her past who might want revenge or something. There has been a long list of stepfathers and boyfriends in her life, and unfortunately she has been victimized by more than one."

"Do you think she might have gone to an abortion clinic?" Tracy asked. "Her mother told me that she gave Calista the money for an abortion. She talked about abortion as if it was just having a parasite or a wart or something removed."

All three adults turned their attention to Tracy. "Tracy, when did you talk to Calista's mother?" Alex asked.

"Oh, I forgot to tell you," Tracy answered. "Um . . . I kind of . . . accidently called her . . . on Calista's phone. I was just going to use it to call home—but I didn't know how to use it. Jordan said to push the button with the green phone icon, and I pushed it twice—her mother must have been first on her contact list. When her mother answered, well, I sort of . . . well . . . I didn't know what to do except talk to her. I'm sorry. I know I shouldn't have used Calista's phone, and I sure didn't mean to call her mother . . ."

"That is a major breach of confidentiality. What were you thinking?" Sadie accused. "Tracy, you ..."

Kathryn interrupted, "Sorry Sadie, but I think we should focus on finding Calista first. Alex and I will deal with Tracy's violation later. Sadie, you were going to look over Calista's files, I think that is a great idea and you should get right on it. Tracy, you can come with me. I have an idea about where she might be."

Sadie started to say something, but didn't. Kathryn felt a pang of guilt for interrupting her friend—again—and taking over the leadership of a situation—again. It was a bad habit that she had, and it was rude and unprofessional. She owed Sadie an apology—later.

As she drove, Kathryn was praying that they would find Calista before it was too late for her unborn child. She knew that legally there was nothing she could do to prevent the teen from getting an abortion, even though Calista had asked to be placed with a pro-life foster family.

This was a neighborhood Kathryn knew well. She prayed fervently that Calista would not be inside the clinic on the corner. Just driving past that place always dredged up emotionally charged memories that she would just as soon forget.

Halfway down the block was the grand old Victorian mansion that had been willed to the local League for Life chapter by one of its founding members, Grace Bowman. It was now a residential crisis pregnancy center called the House of Grace. Kathryn had been working there as a counselor for several years.

Grace Bowman was a widow with no children of her own when the abortion clinic opened up less than a block away from her big empty house. She was already an active supporter of the pro-life movement. She knew that many women chose abortion instead of adoption or parenting because they didn't know of any other options. So she opened her home to young women who just needed a place to stay and be nurtured so they could give life to their babies. She often said, "There is no such thing as an unwanted child, only unwanted pregnancies." Under her leadership, there was no 'sidewalk counseling' or picketing at the abortion clinic. There were no threats of violence against the doctors or staff. The team members prayed every day for God to send the women who needed help, and he always delivered.

Kathryn's memories and silent prayers were interrupted when Tracy shouted, "Look, Mom! She is sitting on the bench in front of the Grace House." Kathryn breathed a silent "*Thank you!*" as she parked the car. She handed her cell phone to Tracy and asked her to call home and let the others know the lost had been found.

Kathryn got out of the car and walked slowly to the bench. "Mind if I join you?" she asked.

"It's a free country," Calista mumbled without looking up.

"So I've heard." Kathryn sat down, and the two of them sat in silence. Tracy came up from the car and handed the phone back to her mom. She stood awkwardly until Kathryn patted the spot on the bench on her other side. The three sat in silence. Tracy wondered if this was a counseling technique that her mother frequently employed.

Chapter Seventeen

Tracy fussed with the hem of her t-shirt for at least five agonizingly slow minutes before she broke the silence. "Calista, I am so sorry for what you are going through. But I hope you can believe that I had nothing to do with that Facebook page."

"I don't know what to believe, or who to trust anymore. A few days ago, I thought I was finally getting my life together. I had a few more months to enjoy what was left of my high school experience and then I could get myself a cute little apartment and raise my baby. I thought I could do it, I really did."

Calista was silent again, and she started to cry. Kathryn handed her a tissue. Tracy fought the urge to say something just to fill the silence. She sensed that Calista wanted to open up, so she followed her mother's lead to allow the troubled girl to collect her thoughts.

Finally, after what seemed like another eternity, Calista continued. "I don't know what the social worker has told you about my life but it's been pretty messed up. My mom lives in a fantasy world, where she is married to some rich guy, and lives in a beautiful mansion, with nothing to do but plan parties and go shopping. She's been married three times now. Eventually reality busts in on her fantasy, and it all falls apart again."

Calista was sobbing now. "When I was thirteen, Mom met this guy who turned out to be a pedophile. She was so determined to get him to marry her, that she offered to let him sleep with me. That was the first time I got pregnant. When she found out, she made an appointment with an abortion doctor right away. I didn't want to be pregnant but I was scared that an abortion would hurt. She told me I had to go, because having a baby would ruin my life, just like I ruined hers." Calista paused to catch her breath and blow her nose. Kathryn handed her the whole package of tissues.

"I finally agreed to go after she promised that we would be rich and live in a big fancy house where I could have a huge bedroom and my own bathroom. She said having a baby would make me fat and ugly. She promised to take me shopping after the abortion to buy a whole new wardrobe.

"So I had the abortion. And it did hurt, a lot. I was bleeding for weeks afterwards. Mom married the guy, but after a few months she decided that he was not keeping her in the style she had expected to become accustomed to. She thought police officers made a lot more money and she nagged him to try harder to get a promotion. She told him he was lazy and lacked ambition. He got angry about Mom spending his money; she got mad because he wasn't making more money; so they divorced." She paused and looked at Kathryn. "I guess you must think I am very shallow. But when Mom didn't come through with her promises, I ran away with an older boy who said I could live with him at his house. Apparently he didn't check with his parents to see if it was okay with them for me to live there. When I got pregnant again, his parents paid for an abortion on the condition that I leave. So I went back to live with my mom.

"Fast forward past a whole lot more insanity to this pregnancy. This one was my fault. I was living with a new boyfriend, and it just felt so right—like—this is the guy who will marry me and get me out of my mother's fantasy world. And yes, I do appreciate the irony," she said with a wry smile. "We lived together for almost two months. I thought it would be so sweet to have a cute little baby together. He didn't agree. He kicked me out. My fantasies don't turn out so well either. So, I looked up my mom, and I found her living here, with another guy. She didn't want him to know that I existed. She gave me money for an abortion and told me not to call her again."

By this time, Kathryn had her arm around Calista's shoulders, and their tears were mingling. "Oh, Sweetie! I am so sorry! No one should have to go through stuff like that! You just go ahead and cry—let it all out. Then we will go get ice cream."

Chapter Eighteen

Kathryn's favorite of the Wilson Family Adages was #5: "*When all else fails, get ice cream.*" Over a round of double chocolate fudge cones, which Kathryn let them eat in the van ("just this once, because none of the little ones are here") and because it gave them privacy to talk and cry. Kathryn asked Calista what she was thinking about the baby.

"I just don't know anymore. I am starting to realize how much I don't know about being a parent. I thought I was ready, but I guess I proved how irresponsible a parent I already am by drinking and, just in case you don't already know, smoking pot. I mean . . . I knew that it was wrong, but I was only thinking about myself and having a little fun before I have to grow up and be a mom. I never even thought about how it could harm my baby. Like, how the twins at your house are so small and they cry all of the time. Have I already done that to my baby? What kind of mother could I be?

"I think that you have already come a long way towards being ready to be a parent," Kathryn said.

"What do you mean?"

"You just put your baby's interests ahead of your own, and thought about how your actions could impact his or her well-being. That is a major step towards becoming a good mom."

"Do you really think so?"

"Yes, I do. And as far as your baby's health goes, nobody really knows how much alcohol is safe to drink during pregnancy, so to be safe, we recommend none. I will be honest with you. Depending on how much and how often you drank, the baby's development might be affected. There are many levels of fetal alcohol syndrome. Thomas and Timothy are pretty much the worst cases I have ever seen. Right from birth, you could see by their facial features and their behavior that they were definitely affected by their mother's drinking. Sometimes we don't see the symptoms of FAS until children are in school and they show signs of learning disabilities."

"So my baby might be retarded?"

"We don't use that term anymore, but yes, it is possible."

"Does that mean that I should have an abortion?"

"Why?"

"Well, because it might be retarded, or whatever."

"We don't know that for sure. You should wait until after it is born. Or if we see signs of slow learning in a few years, maybe we could do him in then."

"Okay, you've lost me again Mama Kate."

"If you kill the child before it is born, and it turns out to have been healthy, then you have wasted a perfectly healthy child. Would it not make more sense to wait until after it born so that we know for sure, and then just kill it if it is defective?"

"How could you just sit there and talk about killing a child? Doesn't that go against your religion or something?"

"Yes, it does go against my religion. Very much so. No matter what age or stage, healthy or not, I am against killing children."

"But I am just talking about abortion, not killing children! What do you think I am, a monster or something?"

"I'll take 'or something' for now. I am hoping that you are not a monster. In my humble opinion, the real monsters are the doctors in there who are killing the babies. Now, eat your ice cream, girls, so that we can go home for supper."

Chapter Nineteen

When they got home, Sadie was back—waiting on the front porch swing. Kathryn sent the girls inside with instructions to make grilled cheese sandwiches and tomato soup. She sat down next to Sadie on the swing. "So you think I have gone soft on this one, do you?"

"I was expecting that you would have at least had a conversation about the sneaking out."

"We have had a couple of conversations about the sneaking out. I hope that we will have time for many more conversations about all kinds of things, including the sneaking out. I think that the soft love approach is going to be needed on this one."

"Well—I defer to your wisdom in reaching pregnant teens. You are going to need it."

"I could use a good dose of wisdom for each of the fosterlings. So, where were we in this morning's updates before life jumped in and rudely interrupted our meeting? And speaking of rude interruptions, I apologize for rudely interrupting you earlier. I got bossy again, and I am sorry."

"Apology accepted. You have great instincts, and more than a good dose of wisdom in reaching troubled kids."

"Thank you. So, where are we at with Jeremy's mom? Is she staying clean?"

"So far, so good. She's got a couple of job interviews coming up. She needs to find a steady job, a suitable place to live, and then stay clean for at least another month before we go back to court. In the meantime, we can schedule some supervised visits."

"And the twins?"

"The police still haven't identified the mother. So they will be with you for the foreseeable future, if you can manage them."

"I've been tired lately, but I love having babies in the house. I don't think we should move them to another foster home—it is so hard for babies to bond with new caregivers, especially FAS babies. I can manage until the mother is identified. I assume you will do a search for next of kin to find relatives who want to raise them."

"That would be best. Have you discussed adoption with Calista yet?"

"Not specifically, but she is reconsidering her ability to be a parent in a few months. And do we know anything about the origin of the Facebook page, or the possibility of Calista and the other girls being drugged at that party?"

"I talked to Sara, the school nurse, about it. She contacted the other four girls and their families, and they all told her the same story: their daughters were brought home by the police late Friday night. They had been drinking, they were all heavily intoxicated, and they were all sick for about 24 hours. I looked into the police reports to see what their blood alcohol levels were and made a startling discovery."

"What did you find?" Kathryn asked.

"Nothing."

"What, do you mean the reports were sealed or something?"

"No. There were no police reports. No record of anyone calling about a party, no reports of the girls being escorted home, no blood or breathalyzer test results."

"So what, were the police officers imposters or something?"

"No, the police officers were real. I looked into who was on duty that night. One name I recognized was Constable Charlie Johnson."

"You mean Monica Lutz's step-father? And Monica was the girl that Andrea was suspicious about, because she didn't get sick. She was the one they suspected of calling the police. So would she have called her step-father to come? Why would they have set that up?"

"I connected the dots today when I looked through Calista's files. Remember the step-father who abused her and got her pregnant when she was thirteen?"

"No!" Kathryn felt chills up and down her spine. "That was only four years ago. Didn't he do any jail time?"

"There was never a report or an arrest. Somewhere out there is a doctor who performed an abortion on a thirteen-year-old, and apparently did not ask questions."

Chapter Twenty

-Sixteen Weeks Pregnant

Calista eventually stopped complaining about walking to school with Tracy and Jordan. She balked at first, on the grounds that she should not be walking in her condition. Kathryn informed her that, on the contrary, walking was the perfect exercise for her condition.

It seemed very weird to Tracy that she was walking with someone who just up until a few weeks ago had been her nemesis. For the first couple of days the silence was awkward. When they got within a block of the school, Calista would turn and go the long way around so that none of the 'cool' kids would see her walking with those two losers.

For the first couple of weeks, Calista fell back into her role as Queen Bee. She made fun of Tracy when they were both at their lockers—especially if any of her flock was within earshot, but even Kristen, Joelle, and Andrea (Calista's 'inner circle') could tell her heart wasn't really in the game anymore. When their paths would cross in the hallways, Calista ignored Tracy and Jordan, and hung out with her friends in the popular group. The cool kids for the most part kept their gossip about Calista behind her back, and when she was with them they ignored the fact that they knew she was pregnant. She in turn ignored the fact that she knew they were just pretending to not know that she was pregnant.

But ignoring a pregnancy gets harder to do in the second trimester. By the fifth month, there was no way for Calista to get into a pair of skinny jeans. Foster parents received a clothing allowance that was almost adequate to keep a growing child reasonably clothed, but Kathryn had to apply for an extra allowance for maternity clothes. When the check finally came, she always enjoyed the bonus shopping time.

Calista and Kathryn spent a whole Saturday together at the mall, and they had an enjoyable time, although Calista was uncomfortable about entering maternity stores and wanted to stick to stores that catered to teens. Her one fabulous find was a pair of extra low rise skinny jeans in a larger size than she ever thought she would have to wear. She wanted to pair them with a tunic length t-shirt that would accentuate the increase in her chest size while de-emphasizing the added curves on her hips, but she couldn't find one. Kathryn kept telling her that maternity pants with the stretchy tummy panel would be much more comfortable than low rise jeans, but Calista stubbornly refused to sacrifice fashion for comfort.

During a break from shopping, over a cup of strong black coffee for Kathryn and an herbal tea for Calista, they had a discussion about Calista's wardrobe choices. Calista was complaining that there were no maternity clothes available for the fashion conscious teen.

Kathryn told her it was just as well, since 'fashionable' teen clothes were part of the reason that teens were having sex and getting pregnant in the first place.

Calista took offense to that comment. She spouted the standard 'politically correct' rhetoric that women have the right to wear whatever style of clothing they like. She refused to believe in a correlation between what she chose to wear, and the attention that she got from guys that had so often led to pressure to hook up with them.

Kathryn countered with a psychological approach. "The male brain is wired differently than ours," she explained. "They think about sex a lot more often than we do, especially teen-aged boys. Their brains are flooded with testosterone and they reach their sexual peak at around nineteen. They are also more visually stimulated, and it is difficult for them to concentrate on anything else if there is an attractive young woman nearby with exposed cleavage or belly; or tight, form fitting clothes."

"You mean like my skinny jeans? But they are just stylish—everybody is wearing them."

"Starting any sentence with, 'But everybody is . . .' is not going to work with me," Kathryn said. "That's Wilson Family Adage # 3. There is no one named 'Everyone Else' living in the Wilson residence. You are only responsible for your own choices, but only you are responsible for your choices."

"So then how could you hold me responsible for what the boys are thinking? Isn't that their choice?"

"That is excellent reasoning, Calista! They *are* responsible for their own thoughts and behaviors. I like to explain it with the 'three strikes' approach. A girl who made the decision to wear revealing clothing walks by a guy. If he notices her, and sees what she is or isn't wearing, that's being human and not blind. If he gives her a second glance, that's temptation. If he keeps looking, and thinks about what it would be like to touch her, that's lust. In the Sermon on the Mount, in Matthew 5:28, Jesus said 'I tell you that anyone who looks at a woman lustfully has already committed adultery with her in his heart.' Now that's Ten Commandment territory. The second and third looks are his choices, and you are not responsible for his choices. But you are accountable for the first look.

"Jesus also said that the two most important commandments are to love God and love your neighbor as yourself. That is the Wilson Family Adage #1. If you love the guys at school, not love as in a sexual way but love as in caring enough to want what's best for them, then do you think it is showing love to deliberately wear something that will tempt them to break God's commandments?"

Chapter Twenty-One

That night, after everyone was in bed, Calista asked, "Hey Tracy—you still awake?"

"Yes," Tracy answered.

"You know those 'purity' rings that you and Jordan wear, what's the deal with that? Does it mean that you are going to be like, virginal nuns, and never have sex, or what?"

Tracy giggled and said, "Not exactly! It's a pledge to not have sex until we are married."

"That's like, totally insane! So you've never had a boyfriend, and you won't until you're married? Who does that anymore?"

"Lots of people pledge to wait. Even now, in this millennium. It's not that weird."

"I think it's weird. It's not natural. So is this like, part of your religion, because sex is so sinful and disgusting to you? Do you just make yourself not like guys?"

"No, sex isn't sinful, or disgusting, and I do like guys. It's not that sex is bad, because God invented sex. He designed it to be pleasurable. The only limit He set is that it stays within marriage."

"That is one ginormous limit! So if you don't get married until you are like, thirty or something, you have to wait until then to have sex? That's insane! Nobody does that anymore. In fact, I don't think that people have ever actually done that. I was pretty sure that you were a virgin, but I didn't know that your people were such Neanderthals about sex in general."

"We see sex as an expression of intimacy in marriage. Virginity is a gift that you can only give once. It is too precious to give to anyone besides a marriage partner."

"Well mine was taken by my mom's marriage partner—actually my mom stole it and gave it to him so that he would marry her. And obviously I have given myself to a few others along the way. You can go ahead and save yourself and your precious virginity for another Neanderthal someday, but I live in the real world where sex is something that people buy and sell or steal or bargain with. I'm going to sleep now. Good night, Sandra Dee."

Chapter Twenty-Two

Life at the Wilson's foster home settled back down to the controlled chaos that passed for normal. The twins were still crying a lot, especially at night, but they were growing and starting to crawl. Tracy was sure that they had some sort of psychic bond or twin language or something. It was like one twin would do something adorable to distract the adults so that the other could go make a mess or get into something.

Jeremy's mother fulfilled the judge's requirements to get custody again, so he went to live with her. That meant that there was an empty bedroom, but Kathryn asked the girls to hold off on moving Calista into her own room just yet. She had one of her "Pray for the best but plan for the worst" feelings that the rest of the family had learned to take seriously. She was praying that Linda (Jeremy's mom) would stay clean and sober to be the mother that Jeremy needed.

But unfortunately, Kathryn's sense of God's plan was correct again. Less than a week later, little Jeremy was witness to the most horrific crime a child could ever face. Linda was shot by an ex boyfriend who wanted her to take him back. Jeremy saw the boyfriend drive up on his motorcycle, and hid in a closet, so fortunately the man didn't even know that there was a witness to his crime. After the man left, Jeremy called 911 and an ambulance came, but Linda was pronounced dead at the scene.

So Jeremy came back to live with the Wilsons. Alex and Kathryn applied to adopt him. The police advised them to have the adoption papers sealed so if the boyfriend ever found out Linda's son witnessed the crime it would be close to impossible to track the boy.

Chapter Twenty-Three

-Twenty Weeks Pregnant

Calista's "Locker Stalker" continued to leave messages on coat hangers. They were always left inside the locker, with no signs of the lock being forced open. Calista changed the combination several times but the messages didn't stop coming.

One Sunday afternoon Alex asked Calista to bring out all of the notes and spread them out in order on the kitchen counter. He rounded up the family for a brainstorming session.

The notes were always printed in large, bold red letters and attached to a wire coat hanger. There had been one or two a month. When lined up in order, the messages read:

> "*Here, you might need this. Those Wilson Neanderthals won't give you a choice.*"

"You've done this twice before. It's no big deal. Just make an appointment and get it done."

"Don't listen to those Bible Thumpers. They will force you to give up your education and social life and spend the next eighteen years in slave labor."

"Why are you still pregnant? You are going to get fat and ugly if you don't get rid of it now."

"It's your body—your choice! Don't let anyone take away your right to a safe, legal abortion!"

"Better have that abortion soon! Second trimester abortions can have more complications."

"Ok, folks," Alex declared dramatically. "I have called this meeting of the best and brightest Wilson family (and honorary Wilson family) brains to storm through the evidence in the case of the *Locker Stalker.* Your mission, should you choose to accept it, is to identify the person or persons who left these notes in Calista's locker. Think about motive, means, and opportunity."

"Who would stand to gain if Calista was to have an abortion?" Kathryn asked.

"I can't think of anyone who would get anything whether I have this baby or not. My mom doesn't want to be bothered by any more children in her life. But she would have no reason to put messages in my school locker."

"Could it just be someone who is very pro-abortion and doesn't want anyone to give birth? Or maybe a hero type who wants to solve teen pregnancy by getting them all to go get abortions? Kind of like the opposite of a pro-lifer?" Tracy suggested.

"I think it is more personal than that. There are three other girls in our school that I know of who are pregnant," Calista mused. "None of them are getting messages in their lockers."

"Calista?" Jeremy tugged on the girl's sleeve. "You won't listen to them, will you?"

"Listen to whom?"

"The bullies that want you to kill your baby. You won't listen to them, will you? I think you will be a good mom."

"Oh, Jeremy!" Calista gave the little boy a big hug. "No, Sweetie, I won't listen to the bullies. I am not going to kill this baby."

Chapter Twenty-Four

-Twenty-Two Weeks Pregnant

Calista gave up on the attempt to hide her pregnancy. Her entourage was reduced to only three or four loyalists. Several girls who used to follow her were confused and keenly disappointed that Calista did not exercise her right to have an abortion. They blamed Tracy and her Neanderthal anti-abortion parents who refused to let Calista get an abortion (they assumed).

The flock of high school boys who had been fawning over Calista and jostling to be her next hook up had moved on once her pregnancy started to show.

Eventually Monica gave up her struggle to win Calista's friendship and be accepted as one of the cool kids. She went back to hanging out with Tracy and Jordan, and eating lunch with them at what she considered to be the 'losers' table in the cafeteria.

Tracy tried very hard to be kind and polite with Monica, but the girl's negativity level would make a potted plant wither and die. She wanted to gossip, and she was very envious of Calista. They had almost the same conversation every day:

Monica would ask, "So what is Calista planning to do with the baby?" And Tracy would reply, "I am sorry, but I can't answer questions about Calista." Then Jordan would say something like, "Why are you even here with us? You know Tracy can't tell you anything about Calista! Why don't you go over and ask her yourself?"

At which point Monica would get all up in a huff, and say, "Well, I won't stay if I am not welcome here!"

Jordan would come back with something like, "Then why are you still here?"

Then Tracy, ever the peacemaker, would say something like, "Girls—both of you, just sit down and eat lunch. Calista and her entourage are ignoring their salads and bean sprouts. They are pointing at us and laughing."

To which Monica would reply, "Of course they laugh at us! They are the cool kids, and this is the losers' table. If I were sitting over there, I could be laughing with them instead of being laughed at."

Jordan really lost it one day when Monica said that. She stood up and said, "Monica, look around you. You pretended to be someone you are not in order to impress people you don't even like. You obviously know that they don't like you, but still you are insulting the only people who try to be nice to you." She looked over at Tracy for confirmation and Tracy nodded just a little as she looked over at Monica and tried to see her as God saw her—a lost lamb in need of love and compassion.

Jordan continued her tirade: "We've been trying to be nice to you, and love you like Jesus loves you, but you don't recognize 'nice' when you see it." Jordan noticed then that the decibel level in the room had dropped considerably, and most of the eyes were on her. "You folks enjoy the rest of your lunch, now," she said as she sheepishly sat down.

Only then did Jordan realize that Monica was crying. Tracy had her arm wrapped around Monica's shoulders, and Monica was getting the sleeve of Tracy's sweater soaked. "I am so sorry. I am sorry for all of it. I didn't want to do it." Monica stood and collected her stuff.

"What do you mean, sorry for all of it?" Jordan searched Monica's face, and then looked over at Tracy, who shrugged her shoulders. "What did you do?"

"I can't tell you. He made me promise. He'll be mad if I tell."

"Who will be mad?"

"My step-father. He made me do all of it. I am so sorry! I need to go," Monica said as she ran out of the room.

"Do you know . . .?" Jordan asked.

"Not a clue," Tracy answered.

Chapter Twenty-Five

The Wilson home was quiet. The police had finally matched Thomas and Timothy's mother to a missing persons file. Once she was identified, they were able to locate her parents. Unfortunately, they had to deliver the bad news that their missing daughter was in fact deceased, but the good news was that they had two young grandsons. So Timothy and Thomas were adopted by their biological grandparents. They would grow up in a big family with lots of cousins to play with.

The house always seemed so empty to Kathryn when a fosterling left. No matter how long or short their stay had been, she had to get through a grieving process when they were gone. She wondered if she was getting a bit too old for fostering. She had always been so energetic and thrived on being needed. For the first time in many years, the nursery was empty. With no babies in the house, Kathryn should have been able to 'sleep like a baby'. Instead, she was restless at night and exhausted during the day.

Tracy no longer had to share her bedroom with Calista. Jeremy moved upstairs into the room vacated by the twins, and Calista moved into Jeremy's vacated room. Alex removed the temporary wall in Tracy's room, so she got her old space back.

Calista's baby was due in April, just two months away. She was excited and nervous and terrified. She was starting to consider adoption. Living in a house with two babies had been a bit of a crash course in parenting, even though she had not been the one responsible for their care.

Alex and Kathryn told Calista that they would support her in any way that they could. If she chose adoption, they would walk her through the legal process. If she chose to keep her baby, she was welcome to stay for up to six months while she worked out a plan for independence as a single parent.

Nesting instincts kicked in for everyone. Alex got a pail of pink paint and one of blue, and offered to paint Calista's room as soon as the baby was born. Kathryn invited Calista to look through the baby clothes and furniture in the storage room and pick out whatever she thought she might like to use.

It was like the whole household was taking a seventh inning stretch; as if they knew they needed a breather to prepare for the next barrage.

Chapter Twenty-Six

The next barrage came on a Monday morning, when no one was expecting it. Calista and Tracy had finally made peace as locker neighbors. The queen bee role just didn't fit Calista anymore. She had outgrown it like a pair of skinny jeans. The proverbial tiara was passed on to Andrea, who quickly mastered the art of working a school hallway like a red carpet, with her own entourage in tow. Monica was not included.

Calista walked to school with Tracy and Jordan, and the three of them were a bit late, as Calista had to stop twice: once at the corner store and again at a coffee shop to use the ladies room. So the hallway at school was almost empty when they got to their lockers.

Tracy's startled gasp reverberated in the empty hallway. Someone had ransacked the inside of her locker! All of her pictures of cute little puppies and kittens had been roughly slashed and splattered with red paint. The neatly stacked books and supplies were strewn about, pencils broken, paper torn out of binders, and splotches of red paint covered her books and gym shoes. The now familiar wire coat hanger with its red lettered message felt more intimidating now that it was addressed to her. In formidable bold all caps, it read: "EVERYONE has the RIGHT to CHOOSE. MIND your own BUSINESS!"

"Now that's just rude!" Jordan remarked, startling her best friend who had forgotten that she was there.

Calista had not been neglected by her locker stalker. The interior of her locker had been similarly defaced. Someone had drawn pregnant bellies on the pictures of fashion models, adding facial and body hair in inappropriate places. The red lettered message in her locker read: *"It's not too late. One little snip, and you have your life back."*

"What's that all about?" Jordan asked.

"I think it's a reference to partial-birth abortion," Tracy said.

"What is that?" Calista asked. "I've never heard of it."

"It's the method they use for late term abortions," Tracy explained. "They either induce labor with drugs, or they use seaweed rods to dilate the cervix. The fetus is partially delivered, feet first, then the body and arms until just the head is still inside. The abortionist reaches in with scissors or another sharp instrument to snip or puncture the brain stem so that a dead baby will be delivered.

If the cervix isn't dilated enough to pull the head out easily, the doctor uses a suction curettage device to suck out the brain so that the head can be removed more easily."

"That is absolutely horrifying!" Calista said. "Do they really do that?"

"Yes they do," Tracy said. "The difference between an abortion and a murder is whether or not the baby's whole body is outside of the mother's body when it dies. In cases where the bodies of newborn babies are discovered, the cause of death is not as important to the investigation as the question of whether or not the baby took a breath before dying."

The vice principal, Mr. Keller walked by just then, and he stopped to ask why the girls were not in class. Suddenly, he turned several shades of red and lowered his voice. "Um . . . Calista? You seem to be bleeding . . ."

"No, it's just red paint that someone splattered . . ." Tracy began. Then she noticed where Mr. Keller was looking. "Oh, Calista—you are bleeding, a lot!"

"I think I had better call 911. Tracy, Jordan: why don't you take Calista to the girls' bathroom? I will send Mrs. Belanger to help you."

Chapter Twenty-Seven

-Twenty-four weeks

By the time Sara Belanger (the school nurse) got to the bathroom, the girls were sitting on the floor. The red puddle under Calista was growing. Calista said, "I think my water just broke."

"And so it has," Sara confirmed. She wrapped a blanket around Calista and asked, "Have you felt any contractions yet?"

"Who-a-a-o-oh!" Calista exclaimed. "Now I have!"

"Okay, remember your breathing. Take long, deep breaths. Jordan, could you go and watch for the paramedics please? Direct them in here."

"What should I do, Mrs. Belanger?" Tracy asked. "On TV, they always tell the husband to go boil some water."

"I think they just say that to give a nervous husband something to do if he is hovering and not helping. You can give me a hand getting these wet jeans off Calista, and then you can find a plastic bag or something to put them in for her."

"I was just going to burn them along with the rest of the maternity clothes. And I am never, ever having sex again!"

"Okay, I think we are having a baby today! And here comes the cavalry," Sara said as the paramedic team came rushing in with their gear.

"Who is this 'we' that you speak of, Mrs. Belanger?" Calista moaned as another contraction had her doubled over in pain. "I don't see anyone else here with wet jeans and labor pains!"

The paramedic team expertly scooped up Calista and set her gently on a gurney. They had a whispered conversation with Sara, and then she turned to Tracy. "Please call your mom and Sadie Nelson, and see if they can get ahold of Calista's mom. I'm going to ride in the ambulance with Calista. We'll meet up at the hospital."

Chapter Twenty-Eight

Tracy had to wait more than an hour for her mom to come to the school to get her. Kathryn was working at the Grace House that morning, and she was in a counseling session when Tracy called. As per protocol, Kathryn's cell phone was off, and the office staff would not interrupt a counseling session. When her mom finally got to the school, Tracy complained about missing the action. Kathryn assured her that babies take hours to be born.

"But this baby isn't due for another three months! Can it survive if it's born this soon?"

"It is possible. You were two months premature. It was touch and go for the first few weeks in the NIC unit, but your father and I got to take you home on the day that you were due to be born."

"I didn't know that, Mom. How come you have never told me that?"

"It is a long, complicated story that I planned to tell you when the time was right. That isn't now."

"Okay, but I am holding you to your word that you will tell me as soon as we can breathe again."

When they got to the hospital, Sadie Nelson and Sara Belanger were sitting in the front lobby. Kathryn and Tracy went over to them to find out what was going on.

"Any news yet?" Kathryn asked.

"Unfortunately yes, but not good news," Sadie replied. "Calista was in labor for less than an hour, but the baby was stillborn. The doctor said he likely died a few days ago."

"It was a boy?" Tracy asked.

"A perfect little boy," Sara said. "He weighed less than a pound, but he was a beautiful baby. Ten fingers, ten toes, and the face of an angel. It's just so sad!" The school nurse bowed forward, with her head in her hands, and began to weep. Kathryn handed her a pack of tissues. When she regained some composure, she continued. "I don't know if Calista told you this, but she and I have met a few times to talk about adoption. My husband and I have been trying for years to have a baby. We had a meeting planned for tomorrow with Calista and Sadie to meet my husband and discuss the legal steps for private adoption."

"Oh Sweetie, I am so sad for you," Kathryn put her arm around Sara's shoulders. Tracy wasn't sure if she should interrupt, but she really wanted to see Calista. She shifted her weight and looked around.

Sadie moved her purse and briefcase to make room for Tracy to sit down. "Calista's mom is in with her now, so we came out here to give them some space."

Tracy was thinking that maybe Calista might welcome some space between herself and her mother. This pregnancy was the reason Calista needed the protection of a foster family. She wondered if Calista might be welcomed back home now that the baby was dead. And she suddenly realized that she would miss Calista. If anyone had asked her a few months ago if she could ever be friends with Calista Dubois, she would have said there was no way.

Feeling awkward and restless, but not wanting to interrupt, Tracy decided to stretch her legs a bit. "I'm just going to go find a washroom," she whispered to her mom. Kathryn nodded. Sara was still crying.

The ladies' room was unoccupied when Tracy went in. She tried to quiet her mind to pray for Calista. Someone came in while she was there and said "Hello." Tracy was startled, but soon realized that the woman was on the phone. And she recognized that voice: Calista's mother! Tracy didn't want the woman to catch her eavesdropping but it was too late to sneak out unnoticed. She quietly lifted her feet.

"No, she didn't have an abortion, the kid just died on its own. It happens sometimes. Maybe it had something to do with the other two abortions. No, I don't owe you any money. The job was to convince her to get an abortion. Leaving messages on wire coat hangers in her school locker? What were you thinking: that she would use one of them to try this at home?"

Now Tracy definitely didn't want Marcelle Dubois to know she was there. It wasn't like she was purposely spying or anything. It was a public restroom. She couldn't help it if someone came in and thought the room was empty.

"Yes, the pregnancy was terminated, but not because of anything you did. The fetus was already dead before she opened her locker. Yes, that is what the doctor said. Yes, the doctors can tell when it died. Maybe the mess you made rattled her, but it wasn't the reason she went into labor. You did not do the job that I hired you to do, so I don't have to pay you."

Now Tracy was almost holding her breath and praying hard that the woman would leave before noticing her.

"How should I know when the old lady is going to croak? Yes she is old and sick, but we only have two months left. No, I do not want you to go to France! Charlie, no! Don't you dare! You would get caught and then I would have no chance."

What on earth was Calista's mom talking about, and to whom? Just then Kathryn came into the room. Marcelle quickly ended the call.

"Sorry," Kathryn said. "I'm just looking for my daughter."

"No problem." Marcelle said. "There hasn't been anyone here since I came in."

Kathryn and Marcelle didn't know each other; they had never met! And then, "*Praise the Lord!*" they both left the room! "*Thank you, God!*" Tracy let herself breath, but counted to fifty before she let her feet down.

Tracy tried to look nonchalant as she exited the ladies' room. Kathryn, Sadie, and Sara were standing together in the hallway, talking quietly.

The concern on Kathryn's face melted into relief when she saw Tracy. "There you are! When did you . . . ?"

Tracy silently shushed her mom as she scanned the crowded foyer. "Did anyone see Calista's mom leave?"

"Yes," Sadie said. "She just left. That's why your mom was looking for you. We are going to see Calista now."

"What's going on here, Tracy?" Kathryn asked.

"Huge news," Tracy whispered. "But not here. You never can tell if someone might be listening in."

Chapter Twenty-Nine

Calista was only allowed two visitors at a time. Kathryn and Tracy went in first. Calista's tear stained face brightened a bit when she saw them.

"Tracy, Mama Kate! Am I ever glad to see you!"

Kathryn went in for the hug. "Oh, Sweetie! I am so sorry!"

Tracy awkwardly joined them in a group hug. Her mind was reeling. "*How much should I tell them, Lord?*" she prayed. *"And when?"*

"It was a boy!" Calista sobbed. "A beautiful, perfect, tiny baby boy! He wasn't a glob of tissue, and he was not an 'it'! He was my son!"

"Oh, I know Sweetie!" Kathryn said. "Did you get to hold him yet?"

Calista started to wail. Tracy was a bit embarrassed for her. Was it okay to make that much noise in a hospital? Kathryn didn't seem to be bothered by it. "Th...the nurses br...brought him t . t . to m..me. He was wrapped in a b ...blue blanket, and . . . and . . . and my mom . . ."

Tracy had been prepared to see tears, but she was caught completely off guard when Calista's wailing turned suddenly to seething anger. "And then my mother came in, and saw the nurse handing him to me, and she yelled at the nurse, 'Get that vile thing out of my daughter's sight!' The nurse was so shocked, she took him back and ran out of here.

"Then Mom told me to get dressed and go home with her, and I don't even know where or with whom she is living now! She actually expected me to just hop out of bed after delivering a baby—I know he was small and premature and everything, but still . . ."

Calista's voice got quieter and deeper. "And then, just for good measure, she told me that this was for the best. Now I can finish high school without a kid in tow, and I can have the life she always dreamed of. But that wasn't the worst. Oh yes, it gets worse! She said that it should be easy enough to lose the weight now, so men will still find me attractive, as long as I was careful not to get stretch marks! The absolute, irrefutable gall of that woman!"

Calista laid her head back heavily on the pillow, exhausted and spent. Tracy looked over at her mom, waiting for her to jump in and tell Calista how wrong it was to be so angry and that she should be the first to offer grace and forgiveness. But she didn't! She just sat beside Calista, wiping the sweat off her brow with a cold cloth, and—Tracy couldn't believe her ears—her mother was humming!

Tracy felt herself getting angry now, but immediately chastised herself for feeling that way. Who she was mad at? Calista? Mom? Calista's mom?

Calista's mom! Tracy had totally forgotten the phone conversation in the bathroom! She looked over at her mom, still humming and stroking Calista's hair. She decided now was not a good time to bring up the subject, especially after a nurse came in to give Calista a sedative. She was quiet now, and looked almost asleep. Sadie and Sara peeked in just to express their sympathy. They both needed to get back to work.

Tracy tiptoed out of the room. She doubted that her mom would even notice that she left. Wait, was she feeling jealous now? That emotion surprised her too. She couldn't remember ever being jealous of a fosterling. Sure, they took up her parents' time and energy, they took up space in the house, and her mom kind of took it for granted that she would help with housework and cooking and babysitting, but Tracy had never given much thought to how she felt about helping her parents with the fosterlings. Was she being exploited? Used as slave labor? After all, it was her parents who made the choice to be foster parents. She didn't have much say in the matter.

Wow! Epic wow! So many strong emotions were flowing through her brain all at once! It was like holding one of those origami pinwheels in the wind and watching the four blades go round and round. Sadness, anger, guilt, and jealousy—where was all of this coming from?

Tracy didn't know what to do with herself. Going to the bathroom to be alone to pray was usually her go-to solution for any problem, but after this morning's eavesdropping episode, she was feeling a bit skittish about going into a public bathroom again.

Wandering down the corridor, lost in her thoughts, Tracy didn't even notice her dad until she bumped right into him!

"Hey Pumpkin!" he said, scooping her into a big bear hug. "Your mother is wondering where you wandered off to."

"So she finally noticed that I left," Tracy mumbled, with a little more spite than she had intended.

"Whoa there, Pumpkin! Where is this coming from?"

Tracy's face softened. "Dad, I need to talk to you about something. It is really important. Like, ice cream important. Do you think it would be okay if we just went to see Calista for a few minutes, and then hit the Frozen Delight?"

Chapter Thirty

"I know that Mom and I don't tell you nearly often enough how much we notice and appreciate what you do and how much you give up without complaining, at least, not complaining too much," Alex said over a hot fudge sundae. The Wilson Family Adages had been Kathryn's idea, but he fully endorsed them, especially #5. There was nothing like a big bowl of ice cream with hot fudge and whipped cream to soothe even the most savage of teenaged souls, or the souls of their parents and guardians.

Tracy had a gentle soul, and she rarely complained, but every now and then she needed to vent a bit of teenage angst over a strawberry shortcake delight. "I can't really explain why I got into such a snit today," she said as she dug out a particularly luscious-looking red berry. "I mean, I do feel really bad for Calista. I know I have the most wonderful parents in the world, and it doesn't normally bother me to have to share you and Mom. It did throw me for a loop when Mom informed me that I was sharing my room with Calista Dubois. But then she turned out to be a lot nicer than I had ever imagined, once you get past the Queen Bee."

"You have had more of an influence over Calista than you give yourself credit for. A lot of the change I have seen in her has been the result of following your example."

"Do you really think so? I don't think she even likes me very much."

"Maybe not at first. At first, I don't think she was capable of liking, never mind loving, anyone, especially herself. But she has changed a great deal since coming to our home. That is due in large part to the example of you and your mother."

"Well, I will have to give that some thought. But there is something huge that I don't know how to deal with. It involves a conversation that I accidently overheard."

"That sounds serious. Is this a 'sit in the van for privacy' discussion topic?"

"Yes, good idea. And thanks for the ice cream, Dad. It's been awhile since we have done a Father/ Daughter ice cream run."

Once Tracy and Alex were comfortably settled in the van, Tracy told her father everything she could remember from the one sided conversation. He wrote it all down on one of the yellow legal pads he always kept in abundant supply in his briefcase. Then they tried to figure out what it was all about.

"Okay, what do we know for sure?" Alex wrote the heading "Facts" on the lined yellow paper.

"The person in the restroom making a phone call was Marcelle Dubois, Calista's mother," Tracy offered.

Alex wrote "Speaker: Marcelle Dubois, one side of conversation overheard in public restroom."

"She was making a big deal out of the fact that Calista's baby died of natural causes, as opposed to an abortion."

"Did she say the name *Calista*, or was that assumed?"

"Now that you mention it, I don't think she said the name. But I think there was enough supporting evidence to substantiate. The speaker was Calista's mother; she was talking about someone who gave birth to a stillborn child, as opposed to having an abortion. Who else could she have been talking about?"

"It seems obvious to us that she was talking about Calista, but to call something a fact . . ."

". . . it has to be able to stand in a court of law, beyond reasonable doubt." Tracy interrupted.

"I see I have taught you well, young grasshopper. So what verifiable facts can we deduce from this one sided conversation?"

"She said that she didn't owe any money to the person she was talking to, because he or she did not complete the job as per the stated outcome; which was to persuade Calista to willingly have an abortion. Then she scoffed at the idea of leaving messages on coat hangers in a school locker. Dad, do you know what this means? Calista's Locker Stalker is someone hired by her mother to convince her to have an abortion! Oh, and Marcelle Dubois threatened to kick Calista out of the house for refusing to abort this baby!"

"Do we know why? That would establish motive."

"No. Even Calista doesn't know why. Plus she is sure that any reason her mother would give would be a lie, anyway."

"Okay, for now we leave motive blank." Alex wrote the word 'motive' as a heading, and put a question mark on the first line under it.

"I don't think 'means' or 'opportunity' will be easy to figure out either," Tracy mused. "We are looking for someone who knows how to open a combination lock and has access to a public school. This is so depressing! The conversation that I overheard doesn't really help to solve this mystery at all."

"I wouldn't say that, Pumpkin. I think there is a lot more information to glean here yet. Didn't you say that Marcelle called the person Charlie, and told him not to go to France?"

"Oh, yes, I did say that. And there was the part about a sick old lady having two more months to croak." Tracy strained to remember everything she heard that morning, and to make sense of it all.

"Oh, oh, Dad! I don't know if this is significant or not, but the note from this morning was printed in a different font than the other notes. The letters were still red, but a different shade. And this time, my locker was opened as well, with a message specifically to me, and both of our lockers were ransacked. Do you think maybe today's message was from a different person than Calista's Locker Stalker?"

Alex suddenly got very serious. "I think it's time to get the police involved."

Chapter Thirty-One

Alex and Tracy met with a police officer who didn't take the threats to Calista, her unborn child, and Tracy seriously at all. They brought the previous notes from home, and the two from today.

"You don't have a crime to report," Staff Sergeant Williams told them. "This is just kids goofing around. They haven't broken any laws here."

"Seriously?" Tracy exclaimed. "There is no law against breaking into lockers and leaving threatening messages?"

"Afraid not, miss. I agree that this is in poor taste and disconcerting, but not illegal."

"So there is nothing you can do to help us to figure out who is threatening my daughter and a girl in the foster system?" Alex asked.

"No offense, Mr. Wilson, but you people need to accept the fact that when you try to take away people's rights and freedoms and send us back to the days of back alley doctors doing illegal abortions, this is the kind of response you should expect. Asking you to mind your own business and let people make their own choices is not such a bad idea."

Tracy was about to launch into a defense of pro-life values, but Alex got her attention by clearing his throat. "Thank you so much for your time, Sergeant Williams," he said as he shook hands with the officer.

As they exited the building and made their way back to the car, Tracy asked her father why he didn't take a stand and tell the officer what they believed about abortion.

"He already knows what we believe. Do you remember what Jesus told his disciples to do when a town won't listen to them?"

"Shake the dust of the town off their feet as they leave?"

"That's it, Pumpkin. We won't change anyone's beliefs by arguing or debating. Time to get back to the hospital."

Chapter Thirty-Two

Kathryn was still at the hospital with Calista when Alex and Tracy got back. Calista was sitting in a rocking chair, holding a blue bundle. She was in a private room, and there was a tear drop shaped sticker on the door with a drawing of a little angel and the letters "Shhh!" It was the hospital's protocol to warn visitors and staff that the patient in that room had lost a baby.

As they came into the room, Calista put her finger to her lips to 'shush' Tracy and Alex. "Let her sleep," she whispered. Tracy was a bit confused, since she knew that the baby was not sleeping, and was a 'him' not a 'her'. Calista pointed to a chair in the corner where Kathryn was fast asleep. "*Okay, that makes more sense,*" she thought.

Speaking in hushed tones, Calista said, "Mrs. Belanger called and asked if there was anything she could do to help. I asked her if she could pick up Jeremy after school and bring him here. Was that okay?"

"Yes, that was very thoughtful of you, Calista," Alex replied. "He is only ten, and he looks no more than eight; but he has been through more life than most adults."

"The little guy has been quietly fascinated by my pregnancy, and he was so looking forward to meeting my baby. I thought that some closure would be a good thing for Jeremy. Do you think he can handle seeing . . . him? I mean . . . the baby?"

"That is very thoughtful of you," Alex said. "I think he is mature enough, and the closure would be good for him. This baby would have been almost like a little brother for Jeremy. When he gets here I will ask him if he wants to see the baby."

"May I see him?" Tracy asked.

"Would you like to hold him?"

"Would that be okay?" Tracy asked. A nurse who had come in to check on Calista nodded, and got a hospital gown for Tracy. Calista handed the blue bundle to Tracy. She opened the tiny bundle to reveal a baby face with closed eyes as if sleeping. "He is beautiful!" she whispered.

"Mrs. Belanger is putting together a memory box with photos, a tiny lock of hair, his footprint and handprint, and a few other mementos—just to acknowledge that he existed. And do you think it would be possible to have a memorial service at church?"

"Absolutely!" Alex touched the little head. "Do you have a name for him?"

"Brendan Alexander Belanger. He wasn't officially adopted by the Belangers, but the nurse who helped me fill out paperwork said that I could give him their last name anyway. And Alex is short for Alexander, right?"

"It is, and I am honored, thank you, Calista" Alex said.

"Did I hear my name mentioned?" Sara Belanger arrived with Jeremy."

"Yes, you did," Calista nodded to Alex, and he got up to talk to Jeremy, leaving a seat for Sara. "The nurse said that I could give him your last name, Mrs. Belanger."

"You can call me Sara now. We've been through a lot together. And I have more sad news. I had to accompany another student by ambulance to the hospital today, but this one didn't make it. Monica Johnson was found in the girls' washroom at school. There was an empty sleeping pill container beside her. She had a note for Calista in her pocket."

"No way! She left a note for me? Seriously?" Calista took the envelope from Sara, opened it and read the note silently. She looked up with fresh tears. "I can't believe I was so mean to Monica. She really had a harsh life. I never really paid that much attention to her. She was annoying. But here's what she wrote to me:

> *Dear Calista, I don't hate you anymore. You were mean to me, but you were also the victim of an evil pedophile just like I was. Charlie*

Johnson married my mom to get to me. He got me pregnant twice. I have no idea how come he didn't get fired from the police. After he divorced your mom, he married and divorced two other single mothers with teenage daughters before he married my mom.

He sure kept the abortion doctors busy. I can't go through with another abortion, but I don't want to give birth to that monster's child. This is the only way. I prayed for God to take this baby to heaven. I would ask God to forgive me for my sins, but I can't because I will never forgive Charlie for what he did to us. God wouldn't forgive me anyway. Even if suicide isn't a sin, I know that abortion is a sin. I have already killed one baby, and this one will die with me.

I don't know why Charlie was so obsessed with you. He got all excited when he found out that we went to the same school. He was on this deranged mission to get you to have an abortion. I don't know what his deal was. He made me put all of those notes in your locker. I peeked over your shoulder to see the *numbers on your combination lock. He also made me go to that party where you got sick—he gave me roofies to put in your drinks to make you look drunk, so that he could pick you up in a police car and find out where your foster family lived.*

I hope that you have your baby. I am sure you will be a great mom.

Sincerely,
Monica Lutz.
(Please don't let them put that monster's name on my grave. I don't know why my mother let him adopt me.)

Chapter Thirty-Three

There was a stunned silence in the room. Tracy had no idea how long it lasted. It was finally broken by Jeremy who asked, "Was Charlie the bully who wanted everyone to kill their babies?" She hadn't even noticed her dad return with Jeremy.

"Oh Sweetie!" Kathryn knelt down to be at eye level with the small child. "You know a lot about bullies, don't you?"

Jeremy nodded, and then turned to face Calista. "Did Charlie make you kill your baby, Calista?"

"No, Jeremy. This baby died . . . well, because sometimes babies just die. It wasn't anyone's fault. Would you like to see him?"

"Yes," Jeremy said solemnly.

Tracy was still holding the tiny bundle. She sat on a bench and beckoned Jeremy to come sit beside her. Once more she pulled back the blanket to reveal the baby's face.

"What's his name?" Jeremy asked.

"Brendan. His name is Brendan Alexander Belanger." Calista said.

"Brendan Alexander Belanger, you were a wanted baby. Your mom is really going to miss you. I miss my mom too. She's is heaven with you. She was a really nice mom. A bully killed her. Maybe you could ask God if my mom can take care of you. She used to read to me and tell me stories. She could sing really nice too." Jeremy kissed the baby on the forehead, and looked up. "Mama Kate, was that okay? I mean, since I have you and Papa Alex now, my mom needs someone to love, at least until I get to heaven, and I might even be a grown up by then."

"Um, yes Jeremy, I . . . um, I'm sure God would love that idea." Kathryn said while fumbling unsuccessfully for Kleenex in her purse. Calista handed her a box of tissues.

Chapter Thirty-Four

"So Charlie Johnson was Monica's mom's third husband?" Kathryn had that bewildered look that Tracy called "Mom's Mental Math" face. How someone as brilliant as her mother could be so bad at math was bizarre. "I do remember Monica and her family attending our church briefly, quite a few years ago. Monica was in your Sunday school class, right Tracy?" Tracy nodded.

"That's why I was confused the other day in your office, Sara." Kathryn continued. "Monica's parents were Mark and Stephanie Lutz. After they divorced, Stephanie remarried twice. It was her third husband, Charlie Johnson, who adopted Monica. I don't remember her second husband's name, but I was pretty sure it wasn't Johnson."

"It was Jones," Tracy piped up. "I remember wondering why Monica changed her last name to her mom's third husband's name, but not the second one."

Calista jumped into the conversation: "Monica was legally adopted by Charlie," she added.

"Charlie married my mom when I was thirteen. He was my second stepfather. I don't remember my biological father.

"The story my mom always told me was that when she was fifteen, she went to Paris with an American family to work as their nanny. She met and married a rich Parisian boy; his parents threatened to disinherit him unless he had the marriage annulled; and he was so distraught by the situation that he jumped off a bridge, never knowing that he fathered a child.

"I never believed that story, because my mom lies about everything. She lives in a fantasy world. Plus, whenever she told the story, she said that my father drowned in the River Thames, which even I know runs through London, not Paris."

"I like that story, Calista." Tracy said. "You told me that one a while ago, and I remember thinking it was kind of romantic. Except for the drowning part. The River Thames is so polluted. It would have been much more romantic to have drowned in the Seine."

Calista gave Tracy an elbow jab over their ice cream cups. It had been a long day: from the disturbing mess in their lockers; to the loss of little Brendan; and then the shock of Monica's suicide. The doctors wanted to keep Calista in the hospital for observation, so Kathryn, Sara and Tracy took her to the hospital cafeteria to see if they had any ice cream. The little vanilla ice cream cups with the wooden paddles were not nearly as good as the ice cream confections available at the Frozen Delight, but at least it was cold and soothing.

"Calista, did I ever tell you about the time I borrowed your phone?" Tracy asked. Calista shook her head. "It was after you threw your phone at me in the school cafeteria. I'm sorry, but I borrowed it without permission. It was Jordan's idea. She said it would be difficult to ask permission to use your phone when I knew you didn't have your phone because I had it. I was going to phone home, but I accidently opened your contact list and called your mom."

"You called my mom?" Calista laughed. "Did you get the 'No one gave me money to have an abortion, so I had to give up my life to raise a kid' speech?"

"Yes, that is exactly what she told me. That's insane! Doesn't she realize how much it would hurt to find out that your own mother wanted to abort you, that if she had had the money for an abortion you wouldn't be here?" As Tracy said this, she noticed her mother's eyes anxiously sweep the room, and she realized what a serious topic they were discussing in a public space. She lowered her voice, even though there was no one else in sight except the cleaning crew in the kitchen.

Thinking about being overheard reminded her about the phone call she overheard in the restroom. Suddenly her brain made a connection, and she had to fight the urge to shout it out. "I can't believe it took until now to put the pieces together! Mom, do you remember way back to this morning when you were looking for me?" Kathryn nodded, so Tracy continued, "I told you I had huge news, but I didn't want to tell you in a crowded corridor?" The others all followed Tracy's lead and leaned in close to listen. That made it easier for Tracy to remember to keep her voice down.

"I can't believe that I forgot about this until now. I was in the ladies' room this morning, when Calista's mom came in and started talking on her phone. I was embarrassed to be there, but when I heard what she was saying, I was very curious. So I lifted my feet up and tried not to breath."

"So that's where you were hiding," Kathryn commented.

"Yes," Tracy smiled, a little, and went on. "She was talking to someone named Charlie, and arguing about whether or not she owed him money for a job she had hired him to do, and she basically said that the job was to convince Calista to get an abortion. She scoffed at his idea about the wire coat hangers and notes, and said that since the baby died of natural causes, she was not going to pay him."

"Wow!" Calista leaned back. "Just when you think it can't get any weirder . . . is it going to get even weirder, Tracy?"

"Yes," Tracy admitted. "She mentioned an old lady croaking, only two months left, and France. Do any of those ring any bells?"

"No, but I am still trying to process my mom hiring Charlie to convince me to have an abortion. I can't get my head wrapped around why she was even talking to Charlie. I thought it was weird enough that my mom was so determined to get me to abort this baby." Calista looked down and patted her tummy. "I just remembered that he is not in there anymore." A fresh tear slipped down her cheek.

"I think Calista has had a very long day, and needs some rest." Kathryn suggested.

Chapter Thirty-Five

Calista was in the hospital for another two days. Tracy was surprised at how much she missed her. "She's almost like a nice person now," Tracy told Jordan. The two girls were at Tracy's house after church on Sunday. "I still can't imagine us braiding each other's hair, or borrowing each other's lipstick or anything like that. But I'm pretty sure now that we can make it to the end of the school year without killing each other."

"I just can't get over how Calista and Monica shared the same step father. Does that make them step sisters?"

"I don't think so. They didn't have him at the same time. Calista once told me that living with both of my biological parents who are still married to each other is weird."

"I wonder what she would think of my family, with four kids who all share the same bio parents who are still married to each other. Come to think of it, my family is pretty weird too."

"Your family is insane, Jordan. All six of you living in a house with only two bathrooms. That is way beyond weird."

"I agree. Both of you come from weird families," Calista said from the open doorway.

"Calista, you're home!" Tracy jumped up and gave her a big hug.

"Careful! Still a bit weak, don't knock me down," Calista said.

"Oh, sorry! Here, come sit down."

"Thanks. Hi Jordan. I'm glad you are here. There is something I have wanted to say . . . something that I need to tell you . . . to tell both of you." She took a deep breath before continuing. "Okay, I can do this. Before I came to live here, I thought all Christians were frauds and hypocrites, and therefore fair game for mockery. I treated both of you abominably, and I just want to say I am sorry and hope you will forgive me."

Tracy said, "Of course we forgive you!" Then she looked over at Jordan and added, "I guess I shouldn't speak for Jordan, even though we have been best friends for so long that we pretty much share a brain."

"What she said," Jordan added. "Of course I forgive you too! And now that we are all friends, maybe you can introduce me to some hot guys."

"Oh, I don't know, Jordan. I don't think any of the guys I know would be Neanderthal enough to respect those purity rings you two wear. And I can't believe I am saying this, but I am starting to think that being a Neanderthal might be a good thing. I was reading in one of those magazines you brought to the hospital for me about 'second chance virginity' for people who want to start over. I talked to your mom about it, and I've decided to go for it. And look what your mom just gave me!"

Calista showed Tracy and Jordan a silver bracelet with the inscription: "***Pure by Grace***". Tracy said, "Wow! That is much nicer than these rings we got from our youth pastor. Not that I am jealous or anything." She smiled so that Calista would know she was just kidding, although she actually was little bit jealous.

"I still don't know if I can do it, but I think I'm starting to see how waiting until you are married has its advantages. You avoid all of the worries about getting pregnant and the risks of STD's and stuff. So, sorry Jordan. I just don't think I know any guys that I would consider 'hot' who would be good enough for you."

"Just as well," Jordan held the back of her hand to her forehead in dramatic pose. "A life of spinsterhood for me! Such is my lot in life. See ya."

After Jordan left, Calista said, "It must be nice, growing up in a home where nothing bad ever happens to you."

"Is that what you think, that nothing bad ever happens to kids who grow up in Christian homes?"

"Well, no offense but . . ."

"Look, you had an extra huge dose of bad stuff happen to you, and I'm sorry that your childhood and your innocence were stolen from you. I get that your life has been harsh. And I get that my life must look like a cakewalk compared to yours. But bad stuff happens to everyone.

"Jordan's mom has cancer, and Jordan has been doing most of the cooking and cleaning and looking after her three younger siblings. That hasn't been easy for her. And you are not the only one who got pregnant from rape. I did too!"

Calista was visibly taken aback by Tracy's outburst. "Wow, Tracy . . . I . . . I never knew . . . I'm really sorry . . . I guess I misjudged you."

"Everybody misjudges me," Tracy said sadly. "People just assume that I have had this idyllic, ivory tower existence—that I don't know any swear words, that I don't know the facts of life, and that I haven't even been through puberty yet!"

Calista paused and looked at Tracy as if seeing her for the first time. "I really have misjudged you. You are absolutely right—I did see you as naïve and . . .um . . .unsophisticated. And I think I expected your parents to be judgmental prudes whose only joy in life was to make sure that no one ever has fun."

"Yes, and baptized in lemon juice to maintain the facial expression," Tracy made a sour face at Calista and then gave her a little smile.

"You truly are nothing like what I expected. This home is always so peaceful, even when the twins were here. I have never felt judged or criticized. You and Jordan had good reason to dislike me, and yet you have made me feel welcome in your home—even giving up half of your room when I first got here. I feel . . . how can I put this . . . I feel safe here."

"I haven't always felt safe here," Tracy took a seat closer to Calista and lowered her voice. "The kids who come to live here have all been through traumatic experiences; and their problems become our problems. Foster parenting can be dangerous."

"I never really thought about that before, but that makes sense. Jeremy was in a dangerous situation—I saw the precautions your parents had to take to keep the guy who killed his mom from finding him. You know—I've really been self-centered all of my life! In my mind, my problems were always bigger than anyone else's."

"Well then, I guess this is as good a time as any to tell you about a dangerous situation that made my mom and dad seriously consider giving up on foster parenting.

"When I was fifteen, we had a sixteen year old fosterling who had gotten pregnant by date rape. Mom convinced her to report the rape to the police. The police arrested her boyfriend, but his parents paid the bail. He came here to get revenge, and I was the only one home at the time."

Tracy got choked up, and Calista got teary eyed, knowing where the story was going. "I let him in, not knowing who he was, and then, um, yeah, he raped me. I, um . . . I got pregnant, and spent the next nine months pretty much in my room in the basement. The other girl blamed Mom for talking her into reporting him, and she left. We have never heard from her since.

"It took the whole nine months to make up my mind about keeping my baby or choosing adoption. Mom and Dad said they would support whatever choice I made, but I know it would have broken their hearts if I chose abortion. I knew that I couldn't raise the child at my age, even with my parents' help. So I chose adoption." Tracy smiled at Calista, who had tears streaming down her cheeks again. "I had a little girl. She was the most beautiful thing I have ever seen. I knew as soon as I saw her that it would have been wrong to have chosen abortion. How could I have taken her life just because her father was a criminal? I reported him and testified against him and he is in jail now. My little girl was adopted by a super nice couple who couldn't have children. They send me pictures. Would you like to see them?"

Chapter Thirty-Six

April 1st was Calista's eighteenth birthday. Kathryn and Alex had offered to host a big birthday bash, but Calista said that she just wanted to spend the day with the family, including Jordan. Jeremy was trying hard to play 'April Fool's Day' jokes on everyone.

The doorbell rang, and Alex opened the door to discover no one there, just Jeremy's Godzilla toy. An hour later, it rang again, and Tracy opened the door to his T-Rex. When the doorbell rang for the third time, everyone including Jeremy had just come to the table for dinner. Alex told the boy to go answer the door himself this time.

Jeremy went to open the door, and then came running back into the dining room. "There's a man from the bank who wants to talk to Calista," he announced. Alex told him to sit down. "No more April Fool's jokes today. Men from the bank don't make house calls, Jeremy."

"This wasn't an April Fool's," Jeremy insisted. "There really is a man at the door who says he is from the bank and he wants to talk to Calista."

"You can't fool us again," Tracy piped up. "It's after six o'clock and the banks are all closed."

Jeremy was close to tears. "I'm sorry for fooling you before," he said. "But this time it really wasn't me."

Just then a man in a suit and tie, carrying an elegant leather brief case, came into the room and cleared his throat. "Ahem. So sorry to barge in like this." he said, with a light French accent. "But the boy is correct." He handed Alex a business card.

"Please accept our apologies for leaving you standing at the door like that," Alex stood and shook the man's hand before taking the card and examining it. "We thought it was another prank. Sorry for not believing you, Jeremy. How can we help you, Mr....um...Grangier?"

"I don't wish to impose. We don't generally make house calls or conduct business after hours anymore. But I do need to speak to a Miss Calista Dubois."

"That would be me," Calista said.

"Happy Birthday, mademoiselle," the banker said with a nod to Calista. "It is your eighteenth, yes?"

"Yes, thank you—it is. Um, have we met?"

"I do not expect you to remember, but we have met briefly a few times when you were a child. I have been managing your trust account."

"Trust account? You must have the wrong Calista Dubois. My mother would never have set up a trust account for me."

"Ah, yes. Your mother, Marcelle Dubois. She has been receiving a check for two thousand American dollars every month for the past eighteen years from your grandparents, yes?"

Calista looked as puzzled as everyone else at the table. "My grandparents didn't send money to us. They were barely scraping by, on a small farm."

"Oh, no, mademoiselle, not your mother's parents, but your father's parents. You were never told about your father's family?"

"I never met my biological father. My mom always told me some tall tale about his parents threatening to disinherit him if he didn't get the marriage annulled. She said he was from France . . ." Calista's voice trailed off as realization and disbelief fought for control of her facial muscles. "Are you saying that the story was true?"

"That is it, exactly, what I am saying, little one. Your grandfather blamed your mother for your father's death. Apparently it was your mother's idea to elope and run off to London, and your grandfather refused until his dying day to forgive her. Your grandmother insisted that you not be made to pay for choices made by your parents. They were, after all, only children. As I recall, your mother was fifteen and your father eighteen."

"This explains so much!" Calista said. "How my mother never worked, but always had money to buy new clothes for us. She complained constantly about money, but she spent it like water."

"And there's your answer to the question about how your mother got her rivers mixed up," Tracy added. Calista still looked puzzled. "You said it was obvious that your mother made up the story, because even you knew that the Thames doesn't flow through Paris. If your parents went to London to get married, that would explain why your father could have drowned in the Thames."

"I thought for sure she told that story just because my grandparents, my mother's parents that is, would be more willing to accept me if I was conceived in wedlock."

The banker cleared his throat. "Your father's parents also required proof of your legitimacy. Your mother informed them of her pregnancy in typical American fashion, during your father's funeral. She had taken the Dubois family name, and insisted that her unborn child be raised in a manner befitting their station in life."

Calista smiled. "That does sound like something my mother would have said. And all these years I thought she changed her name just to add drama to our lives."

"How undramatic was your mother's maiden name?" Jordan asked.

"Cheryl Brown."

"Not so epic," Jordan said.

"Might I add, little one, it is fortunate that you resemble your lovely mother in appearance only. Despite the appalling lack of manners displayed by your mother, I was contracted to investigate the legitimacy of your mother's claims. Once it was ascertained that you were indeed the legitimate offspring of Charles Dubois, my services were retained to see to your financial well-being, which has necessitated frequent communication with your mother. Upon your eighteenth birthday, the celebration of which I see that I have intruded upon, I am most grateful to transfer my services to you, mademoiselle." The French gentleman bowed slightly.

"My apologies, sir, but—transfer your services to me?"

"Mademoiselle, you cannot be expected to manage the Dubois family estate without a financial advisor on staff."

"I have staff? Are my grandparents . . ?"

"Yes, Mademoiselle, I regret to inform you that your grandparents have indeed passed on. You are the only surviving heir to a rather substantial estate. I have been retained to manage your financial affairs.

"Your grandmother dearly wanted you to come to Paris to live with her, especially after the death of your grandfather. But your mother insisted that you not be informed of your status as heir to the Dubois family fortune until your eighteenth birthday.

"Your grandmother reluctantly agreed to wait until your eighteenth birthday before making contact with you. It meant that she would be almost seventy years old before she would get to meet her granddaughter. But she did insist on adding a caveat to the agreement. If it should so happen that you were to have a child before your eighteenth birthday, this event would have made you an emancipated minor, in which case your mother's legal rights to custody could have been severed.

"I have been in contact with your mother frequently over the years. When I discovered that she took you to have abortions rather than allow you to live with your grandmother in Paris, Madame Dubois was furious, but her hands were tied by the wording of the agreement.

"I suspect that your mother was literally banking on the hope that Monsieur and Madame Dubois would both pass on while she still had custody of you, so that she could manage your inheritance and relieve me of my duties to you.

"Your grandmother was extremely ill for several years. The thought of meeting you gave her hope and strength to go on. She almost made it, but it is with my extreme regrets that I must inform you, mademoiselle, that your grandmother died last week."

Chapter Thirty-Seven

"Now that definitely qualifies as epic!" Jordan exclaimed. The three girls were sitting in the library nook, eating their second and third helpings of birthday cake.

"Epic it is!" Tracy and Calista said at the same time. Tracy looked over at Calista. "It's official!" Tracy laughed. "You have been hanging around us for too long."

"Well if you don't want to hang out with me anymore, I have a little two storied penthouse apartment in Paris, and summer homes in Italy and Wales . . ."

"What? No villa in the south of France?" Jordan asked.

"I would have to consult Monsieur Grangier, but I think he did say something about owning a vineyard in Nice . . ."

"Oh, that's nice," Jordan quipped.

"No," Calista responded. "It's spelled like 'nice' but pronounced 'niece'.

"Jordan is being punny again. Très lame. But it must be nice to have a resort in Nice." Tracy said.

"So what are you going to do with all that money?" Jordan asked.

"What will I do, that is a very good question. Monsieur Grangier just handed me a check for five thousand American dollars and asked if that would be enough to buy myself a nice dress and shoes for the prom."

"Epic!"

"Epic it is!" Calista agreed. "I asked him if I could use it to fix the roof on the Grace Home. Mama Kate said they haven't been able to use the two bedrooms on the third floor because the roof is leaking. I told him about how they take in women who don't want abortions but think they have no other options.

"And I told him how Grace Bowman said there is no such thing as an unwanted child, just unwanted pregnancies. Much as I would love to go shopping for a prom dress and shoes with five thousand dollars, I wouldn't feel comfortable knowing the money could go a long way towards making some less fortunate people's lives easier.

"Monsieur Granger laughed and wrote out another check made out to your mom to fix the roof and whatever else needed to be fixed. It was for two hundred thousand dollars!"

"That's like, epic times infinity!" Jordan said. "You could be like Oprah!"

"I don't think it is quite as much as Oprah," Calista chuckled." But I do have a dream that could actually be attainable now. I want to live in Paris and study fashion design. I could design maternity clothes for fashion conscious women. There must be a way that pregnant teens can dress modestly but still be stylin'."

Chapter Thirty-Eight

April 27th was the day Calista's baby had been due. She spent the day moping around. In the evening, Kathryn found her in the library corner, looking through the books. "Finding anything interesting?" she asked.

"Actually, I was hoping you would come down here tonight. I have a question I have wanted to ask for a while now. It's a sit down question." Calista sat in one of the big comfy chairs, and waited until Kathryn was sitting comfortably before she continued. "Mama Kate, do you think my baby went to heaven? Did he have a soul yet?"

"Yes to both questions. I am sure that he did have a soul already and he is in heaven with Jesus."

"You seem pretty sure of that. Well, um, what about . . . me? Do you think I am good enough to get into heaven?"

"No, you are not good enough, Calista. You won't ever be good enough for heaven."

Calista looked crushed. "Why, because of the abortions? They weren't my fault! Well, the first one wasn't my fault. And there is nothing I can do now to bring those children back—so what are you saying? That there is no hope for me? What happened to that grace that you are always talking about?"

"Oh there is hope," Kathryn said. "And there is grace more than sufficient. But there is nothing you can do to be good enough for heaven."

"Okay, now you are talking in circles again," Calista pouted. "How can there be hope if there is nothing I can do?"

"Can you answer another question first? If you were to die today, and you were met by an angel at the gates of heaven, what could you give as a reason for him to let you in?"

Calista thought for a moment, and then answered, "I don't know. I know I haven't been as good as Tracy, but I didn't have anyone to teach me the difference between right and wrong. I think that I did the best I could under the circumstances, so I think God would see my heart, and know that I am a good person . . . right?"

"I am sorry, but—no. The Bible says that no one is good enough for heaven. We have been born with a sinful nature, so we have to be born again."

"Where did the sinful nature come from?"

"It started in heaven . . ." Kathryn began.

"Really? I though heaven was a perfect place," Calista interrupted.

"It is. God created angels to live there. But one of the angels, Lucifer, became jealous of God, and wanted to be like God. He led a rebellion in heaven, and God booted him and all of the angels who had joined him in this rebellion out of heaven.

"Then God created the Earth and the entire physical universe. He made humans to live on the Earth to care for it. But he allowed Lucifer (whose name was changed to Satan, which means adversary) to go to the first humans—Adam and Eve—and tempt them to disobey God."

"That's the story where they ate fruit from a forbidden tree, right?"

"Right you are," Kathryn continued. "Satan was permitted to tempt Adam and Eve to eat fruit from the Tree of the Knowledge of Good and Evil. He lied to them. He said that if they ate this fruit, they would be like God. Because of his success in tempting them, Satan was granted authority over the humans, and since then all humans are born with a sin nature."

"That doesn't seem fair! Why can't God just free them?"

"That is an excellent question, Calista!" Kathryn said. "God promised all of the people who stayed faithful to him that He would send a redeemer (savior, messiah) to set people free."

"I know this one! Jesus!"

"An excellent student! If I had a gold star, I would give it to you." Kathryn looked up and saw

Tracy coming downstairs. "Hey Sweetie! Did you finish helping Jeremy with his homework?" Tracy nodded. Kathryn got up to leave.

"Don't go yet!" Calista said. "I don't think you finished the story. Isn't there a part about saying a prayer, and getting born again? If I could be born again, I wish I could be born into your family!"

"For real? Would you like to be born again?" Tracy asked. "Are you seriously ready to become a Christian now?"

"Yes, I think so. I mean—I think I am ready. I've been watching your family and comparing it to mine. You guys all love each other so unconditionally and you take care of each other. Then someone like me comes in and you love me too, even when I am puking all over you the first night I got here! If being Christian is what makes the difference between your family and mine, and if there is any way that the bad stuff I have done can be somehow erased, then that's what I want."

"Well, you wouldn't be born again into our family; you would be born again into God's family," Kathryn said. "And God doesn't exactly erase sins, but He will forgive you from your sin and help you to forgive the people who have sinned against you."

"It would sort of be like Calista joining our family," Tracy said. "Because we have all been born again into God's family, we are all one big happy family! It's too bad Jordan isn't here; we could have shown you the 'Sister-Chicks' handshake dance. It's harder to teach without Jordan."

"I think I'll take a rain-check on the dance," Calista said. "But do I have to confess all of my sins and forgive everybody who has sinned against me, and do something about the trespassers? What do I all have to do before I can be born again?"

"Good call on the dance," Kathryn said. "Tracy and Jordan made it up when they were five. But you don't have to do anything before you pray to accept Christ."

"Some people think they have to clean up their lives before God will accept them," Tracy added. "But that would be like not going to the doctor because you are still sick. If you think you have to diagnose and heal yourself before you can go to the doctor, you won't ever go."

"What if I can't forgive everyone? I think I have heard something about God not forgiving you until you forgive everyone."

Kathryn said, "Forgiving is a process, you have to work at it. It isn't an emotion that will just come to you some day. You won't just wake up one morning to discover that your anger is gone and now you feel like forgiving. Also, you don't need an apology from the one who has hurt you. Forgiving someone doesn't mean saying that what the person did to you was okay, and it doesn't mean that you won't call the police if you are being abused or testify against someone in court. It doesn't mean that your trust in that person is restored, or that you will have to go back to an abusive relationship.

"What it does mean is that you release yourself from the bondage of anger and vengefulness that ties you to that person. Sometimes you may be able to rebuild the relationship, but not always. It is something that you do for yourself, not the other person. Sin leaves us wounded, and when we don't forgive, those wounds are allowed to fester in a slime of guilt, shame, anger, vengefulness, and bitterness. When we let God heal our wounds, we still have the scars from our experiences, but not the festering slime. Scars give us character."

"Gross! This story is way more disgusting than I expected," Calista interjected. "Are you sure this stuff is all in the Bible?"

"Yup," Tracy said. "There is a lot of disgusting stuff in the Bible. And we haven't even gotten to the book of Revelation yet."

"So, let's skip the blood, and just tell me—how do I become a Christian?" Calista asked.

"Okay," Tracy replied. She looked to her mom to see if she wanted to lead. Kathryn gave her a 'go ahead' smile, so she continued. "Do you admit that you are a sinner?"

"Do I just say 'yes' or 'no'?" Calista asked. Tracy nodded, so Calista responded with "Yes! I think we all can agree on that one."

"All right then, are you willing to repent—like— turn away from your sins?"

"As far away as I can get!" Calista agreed.

"Now, do you believe that Christ died on the cross and paid for your sins with his blood?"

"I don't really understand all of that yet," Calista admitted. "Is it okay for me to just say I want to believe, and I'll learn that later?"

Tracy looked over at her mom for confirmation. "Yes, Calista, that is very much okay," Kathryn assured her.

So Tracy continued, "Then just repeat this prayer one line at a time if you agree:

"Dear Lord Jesus, I know that I am a sinner."

Calista repeated her words: "Dear Lord Jesus, I know that I am a sinner."

"I believe you came to die for my sins so that I could be set free;" Tracy paused while Calista repeated. Then: "I repent of my sins and ask for forgiveness; and invite you to come into my heart and life," and paused for Calista to repeat. "Then say, I want to trust and follow you as my Lord and Savior, and I am willing to learn all that I can about you. In Jesus' name, Amen."

Calista repeated the last line, and Kathryn and Tracy both chimed in with the "Amen!"

Calista looked up quizzically. "So now do you pronounce me 'one of you' or something?" she asked.

Kathryn and Tracy laughed, and Calista joined in. "I still think you are a weirdo, though."

Tracy laughed and said, "Well now you are one of us, so that makes you a weirdo too!"

Chapter Thirty-Nine

One evening, when Kathryn and Tracy were alone in the cozy library corner, Tracy prayed silently for courage, and began a conversation that she had been rehearsing in her mind for pretty much forever.

"Mom, there is something I have wanted to ask for a long time now, but never found the right time," she began.

"Then this must be the right time."

"Okay, then. Why didn't you and Dad have more children? And why did you get into foster parenting? I know that's two questions, you can answer whichever one you want first."

Kathryn didn't say anything for a long time. Tracy finally looked up, and there were tears streaming down her mother's face. "Mom? You don't have to answer either one right now, or ever. I will still love you."

"I do want to answer both questions. There is something that I have kept from you until the time was right. I just . . . I didn't know . . . Okay. Words, into sentences, make."

Kathryn smiled a little, Tracy smiled back, and Kathryn tried again. "Okay. What I have never told you, what I need to tell you, now that the time is right: I had an abortion."

"Oh, Mom! Is that why you got involved with the pro-life stuff? And the fostering?"

"Yes, and yes. I felt so guilty. You see . . . I wasn't a teen. I was twenty-five years old. I was married. I was on the Pill. I just . . . I just forgot . . . once, to take the pill. Well, okay, I forgot for three days in a row, once. I got pregnant. Your father and I both wanted kids, lots of them. But not just yet. I thought that my career was important. Your father supported me while I finished my masters' degree. I wanted to establish a career as a school guidance counselor, so that when all of those kids were in school, I could have a career to go back to. One where I would work the same months that the kids were in school."

"I can see how that would be a good thing. You would be off in the summer holidays, and spring break and stuff."

"Yes. I was hired by the school division to do exactly what I had trained for. It was my dream job, and I loved it. I worked there for two years. My career was on its way. So then it was your father's turn to go back to law school. Everything was right on track with our ten year plan."

"I didn't know that Dad wanted to be a lawyer. What happened?"

"Well, it was like I said. I missed taking the pill, and I got pregnant before the schedule said I could."

"Wow! I know that Dad likes to make his yearly, and his five, ten, twenty year plans. But I can't imagine that Dad would be angry with you for messing with his schedule by getting pregnant. That's just not like him. Has he changed that much since then?"

"I was too ashamed of myself to tell him. I still can't believe that I ever thought he could be. I just didn't know anything, and I believed my doctor when he said it wasn't really a baby yet, just a bunch of tissue - no big deal. I could be in and out on Friday and back to work on Monday -just as if nothing had happened. So I made the most selfish, short sighted, horrible decision in my life. I made an appointment to have an abortion."

"So you took your experience of having an abortion because you didn't know better, and now you do know, so you counsel women in crisis pregnancies. You teach them what a fetus is, that it is a real baby, and that abortion is really killing a baby, and you help them to learn about their options. So it's really all for good, right?"

"I see that someone has been listening to me all these years. That is exactly what I have been saying. But the most horrible part of the whole mess was that I waited too long to decide. I had an abortion at thirty weeks, and I was never able to get pregnant again."

"I don't get it. Wait, was I adopted?"

"No, you were not adopted. You were the child that I was willing to sacrifice for the sake of my career."

"Wait . . . now I am really confused. So you didn't go through with the abortion . . . or . . . what?"

Kathryn smiled at her beautiful, smart, healthy daughter, whose life was spared by the grace and mercy of a loving Father. Through streaming tears, said, "Tracy, my precious one. You were the gift from God that I didn't deserve. I made the wrong choice between giving you life and just throwing you away, as you so eloquently described it—like having a wart or a parasite removed.

"Do you remember when I told you that you were premature and needed to stay in the NICU for two months? I promised to tell you the whole story when the time was right. Well, the time is right now.

"And do you remember telling Calista that it would be horrible to know that your own mother would have aborted you if she had the chance? It is definitely time to confess, because that is exactly what I did to you, and I am overwhelmingly sorry.

"I have been keeping this secret from you until you were old enough to comprehend what a grave injustice I committed against you. I was ready to give your life as a sacrifice to my own selfish ambitions and vanity.

"But God intervened and gave you back. The amazing and wonderful complication of my abortion was that my baby was still alive. The doctor would not allow the nurses to call 911. He ordered them to take you into the back room to die. But one nurse was horrified. She had heard about the Grace Home, so she grabbed a towel to wrap you in, and put you in my arms, with your umbilical cord still attached, and told me to hang on for the ambulance. Then she ran to the Grace Home and called 911 from there.

"You survived the abortion."

Wilson Family Adages:

#1 - We love God with all our hearts and with all our souls and with all our strength and with all our minds; and we love our fosterlings as if they were our own children.

#2 - We do not gossip about fosterlings. We will respect your privacy and will not betray your trust.

#3 - Everyone Else doesn't live here.

#4 - Grace and Mercy live here.

#5 - When all else fails, get ice cream.

About the Author

Karen Gross has worked in schools, libraries, and museums, but when sidelined for health reasons, she took up writing and discovered her true passion. For the past fifteen years, she has been entering writing contests, writing short stories, blogging, and writing articles to post on content sites. She has about seven hundred articles posted on various websites and blogs. Her wonderful, supportive husband suggested that she focus her attention to one project. This novel is the result.

Karen lives in Canada with one husband, two adult daughters, two cats, and one spoiled little white dog.